WILLIE GIBBS

Don't Walk the Rails

GIBBS PUBLISHING
GPC
CONGLOMERATE

This is dedicated to all who grew up with the legends and folktales of Baltimore City. May those stories—and the memories of the good old days—stay with you always.

"Every city has secrets; urban legends are just the ones that scream the loud-est."

—Anonymous

Foreword

I should tell you this before you go any further.

The worst mistake I ever made was thinking I could look into the dark and walk away unchanged. I thought it would be simple—just stories, just whispers, just shadows. But shadows are never empty. They hold things, and once you notice them, they notice you.

You may believe that evil belongs to other people, other places, distant from your life. That's what I believed, too. Until I found it standing far too close, quiet and patient, waiting for me to give it the smallest invitation.

I won't dress this up with warnings of curses or fate. The truth is simpler: if you go looking, you will find it. And once you do, it will not let you forget. Evil clings. It follows. It waits for the weakest hour of the night, for the smallest crack in your thoughts, and then it slips in.

I wish someone had told me to leave it alone. To close the book, turn away, never ask questions about the shadows. But no one did. And now I can't unsee what I've seen.

So I urge you: tread carefully. Read on if you must, but know that stories are not always confined to the page. Sometimes, in looking too long into the abyss, the abyss learns to look back.

—Gary Winchester

Preface

Legends are living things. They travel by word of mouth, whisper through alleyways, and nestle into the cracks of old city bricks. In Baltimore City, where stories are as layered as the neighborhoods themselves, few tales have endured in the shadows like that of the Bunny Man.

This novel is a work of fiction—but it is rooted in a truth all storytellers understand: folklore matters. The Bunny Man has been passed around for decades, his legend shifting with each retelling—part myth, part warning, and wholly Baltimore. Rather than let this piece of our local lore fade into the background, I wanted to give it new life, a fresh voice that still echoes with the old, familiar fear.

Here, I've re-imagined the Bunny Man's tale not as a dusty campfire story, but as a living narrative—one that blurs the line between the past and present, reality and myth. This book isn't an attempt to explain the legend, but to preserve it, honor it, and—perhaps—keep it watching from the edges of our city streets a little longer.

— *Willie Gibbs*

Acknowledgments

First and foremost, thank you to my friends and family—your constant support, encouragement, and patience made this journey possible. To those late-night listeners, early readers, and honest critics: your belief in my work and vision kept me moving forward even when the path was unclear.

To everyone who ever said, *"You've got something here"*—this book is for you. Your faith in these pages helped bring them to life.

Blood on the Iron

The Carver Vocational Technical High School cafeteria gnawed at the nerves, each fluorescent bulb flickering like the onset of a seizure. Trays smacked onto tabletops in a metallic rhythm, punctuated by the hollow laughter of the seniors who believed themselves immortal. Through the stench of overcooked chicken nuggets and chemical floor wax, Marcus Anderson—Mar-Mar to his chosen—held court in the far corner, his athletic frame hunched over a table where gossip metastasized.

"Listen up, y'all," Marcus said, voice slicing through the white noise. "I'm saying, they found another one. Out by the ACME building. Sliced and banged up. Like, not even the regular way." His hand curled into a vague claw, punctuating the horror with a half-shrug, half-chuckle.

A flock of underclassmen had gathered nearby, feigning indifference while listening with their whole bodies. Tasha Williams, across from Marcus, angled her chin down as she unlocked her phone, brown eyes darting at the screen. She typed "ACME Factory body" with the focus of someone doing research for class.

"I'm just sayin'," Marcus kept on, "what if it ain't no accident? What if all this tied together for real? Think about it."

Tasha's lips twisted. "It's probably fentanyl again, Mar.

Overdose or some botched deal. You realize how many people die on those tracks every year? It's the one place police don't bother to check."

Marcus cracked a grin, teeth flashing like he was daring somebody to check him. "Aight, I feel you. But fentanyl don't explain why they ended up gutted and beat down like that."

Darnell Thompson—D.T. to everyone who'd ever heard him tell a joke—leaned in, the varsity jacket slung from his shoulders like he was born wearing it. "Y'all got it wrong," he said. He glanced around theatrically, as if expecting the walls to lean closer, before dropping his voice to a dramatic whisper. "That's the Bunny Man."

A ripple of groans and laughter. Marcus stabbed his fork into a congealed patty. "Bro, ain't nobody scared of no Easter reject."

Darnell wagged a finger. "Nah, for real. My cousin's boy got chased off the train tracks last summer. Said he saw some dude with a hat, like flaps and all, just standing in the dark. Watching."

Tasha rolled her eyes. "Was he high?"

Darnell shrugged. "Who's not, around here? Anyway, besides the point."

Jasmine Mitchell sat in uneasy silence, retreating inward as laughter rippled around the table—laughter about someone who'd been murdered. She tore at the brittle edge of her bread, fingers working nervously. Her gaze flicked from Marcus to Tasha, then to Darnell, scanning for refuge in faces that offered none. She took it all in, every word landing heavy, leaving its mark.

The rumor had a life of its own. By the next table over, two sophomores already whispered about the "fresh kill." The story unspooled in real time: one said the killer gutted people, another that he left rabbit tracks in the dirt. Marcus watched the infection spread, his smile flattening into calculation.

He turned to Jasmine, voice dropping to a register that only she could hear above the cafeteria's chaos. "You hear anything about this, Jas?"

Jasmine hesitated, eyes glued to her tray. She shook her head, the motion small and apologetic. "Just what you said."

Marcus nodded, satisfied, but Tasha caught the moment and frowned. "She probably heard more than you, Mar. Maybe she's not into the drama."

Jasmine glanced up, and for a moment their gazes met—her fear, his ambition, Tasha's skepticism tangled between them like barbed wire.

Darnell, bored with the lull, launched a balled-up napkin at the next table and leaned back. "Whatever. Bet none of you would make it a night in the ACME building."

Marcus snorted. "Bet your life, D.T.?"

"Only if you're betting yours, too."

"Bet. You down?" He looked at Tasha.

She smirked. "I'll bring my inhaler."

"You don't use an inhaler," Marcus said.

"Exactly," she smiled back.

The first warning bell screeched overhead, scattering the drama like roaches from a light. Students started to stream to their next periods, a tide of restless bodies, but the murder, legend lingered in the stagnant air above the corner table. Jasmine stood last, clutching her tray beneath the unblinking light.

The cafeteria drained of voices and footsteps, leaving behind the echo of Darnell's dare. "Bunny Man's waiting, y'all," he called, the words trailing Jasmine through the door like a specter that wouldn't let go.

She paused in the hallway, listening for a heartbeat that wasn't hers.

Students drifted through the corridor, weaving between lockers layered with half-curled band fliers and campaign posters torn away at the edges. Marcus and Darnell broke ahead, cutting through the crowd with the ease. Tasha followed, sighing like she'd done this a hundred times, while Jasmine slipped behind them, caught in their wake like debris in a gutter. The morning's rumor—the corpse, the myth, the dare—surfaced in scattered whispers, rising and falling as they moved toward their next class. At the stairwell, they paused. The cement bore the scars of years of restless feet, and the banister gleamed with the oily sheen of teenage hands.

From behind, Andre Johnson pulled up, sweat shining on his face from the walk. "There y'all go," he said, voice low but heavy. "Heard you was talkin' 'bout that body they found by ACME?"

Marcus slapped the nearest locker with a bang. "We got all kinds of stories, man, but yeah, that's the one."

Andre's eyes scanned the group. "Police got half the block cordoned off. Yellow tape, the works. They got the tracks locked down, too. This ain't no prank."

Darnell's smirk, "You late bro, we know."

"They ain't pull up in just one car," Andre said, brushing off Darnell like he wasn't there. His voice dropped low, careful, like he was passing off something delicate. "Whole bridge was lit up. Had the dogs out, too. Ain't seen that in a minute."

Marcus's lips curled, excitement and anxiety jostling for space on his face. "That means they're looking for someone."

Tasha folded her arms, textbooks clutched to her chest. "Or

something," she said, voice edged with mockery. "Maybe your Bunny Man's just a crackhead in a hat, Darnell."

Darnell snorted, but the laugh was thin. "Either way, don't none of us want to end up like that body."

Marcus leaned in, eyes locked on the crew. "Y'all still duckin' my question. For real—let's go peep it ourselves. Slide down there tonight. For only a minute. Could be fun."

Jasmine's head snapped up, eyes wide as the gash in her confidence. "We didn't answer because its dumb. Why would we do that?" The words were barely louder than the shuffling feet around them.

Marcus shrugged, all easy swagger. "Because we're not scared. And because maybe there's something out there the cops can't see."

"Or maybe," Tasha said, "we end up like the last idiot who thought he was invincible."

Andre didn't blink—but simply stared Marcus down like he was holding a lit match over gasoline. "This ain't a game, bro."

Marcus gave him a half-smile, half-grimace. "Didn't say it was. All I'm saying, I'd rather know than not. This is our hood, why y'all actin scared?"

Jasmine worried at her nail, zeroed in on a speck lodged beneath the edge until she worked it free. She scanned her nails one by one, and once she was sure hers held up, she lifted her gaze and met their eyes.

"Ain't nobody scared," Darnell said before he jostled Andre who was staring down the hall at the police cruiser idling across the street, visible through a break in the crowd. "You in or out, big man?"

"I'm down," he said, snapping outta whatever zone he was in. "But we gotta move smart. No wildin'."

Marcus beamed, eyes flickering with something colder than bravado. "That's all I ask."

Tasha shook her head. "You're all idiots." But her mouth didn't match the contempt; the corners twitched up, as if she enjoyed the looming disaster.

A security guard shuffled by, eyeing the group like he'd seen this scene too many times. "Let's go, fourth period's on deck," he muttered. The crew started moving again—Darnell tossed Tasha a sly wink, and Marcus gave Andre a backslap that landed with more noise than meaning.

Andre stood beside Jasmine, his bulk crowding most of the hall. He nudged Jasmine with a gentle shoulder bump. She'd had barely said a word.

"Jas, you in?" Marcus asked. The question had teeth, but his eyes softened when he looked at her.

Jasmine's gaze fixed on the linoleum floor, voice a shade above the air conditioner's hum. "Do we have to go at night?"

Marcus smiled, crooked and sincere. "Scary things hide in the dark, right? That's how you catch 'em."

Tasha placed her phone in her back pocket. "I don't see why we can't wait and read about it on Twitter tomorrow. Or let the cops do their job for once."

Andre cleared his throat, slow and steady. "If we're going, we go together. Nobody splits off. No dumb dares."

Marcus smirked. "Hell yeah—that's what makes us a crew," he said, locking it in.

Darnell glanced from Andre to Marcus, and back again, pressure all over his face. "Aight, fine, I'm in," he finally said. "But only 'cause I wanna see Marcus take off screamin' like a lil' kid."

Marcus shot Darnell a half-hearted finger gun, smirking. "That's what I'm talkin' about."

They were walking when Andre glanced over at Jasmine, catching how quiet she'd gone. "Jas, you don't gotta roll if you don't want to," he said.

Jasmine held tight onto her backpack straps. "I don't like the idea of anyone being left behind."

Andre nodded, understanding more than he let on. "We'll stick together. I got you."

Jasmine's mouth flattened, before she gave a small nod. "I'm in," she said, though the words wavered like she wasn't sure she meant them. "But I don't like this. Not at all."

They locked in eight o'clock, right after the corner store's last shift cleared out. The plan was shaky at best: slip across Super Pride's busted lot, squeeze the gap in the back fence, follow the tracks to dodge the cops, and hit the ACME loading dock. In and out—grab proof before anybody's mom lit up their phone. Marcus laid it out like a coach calling plays, his words coming out fast, like the game was already on.

The bell screamed for fourth period, its echo hanging over them as they froze for a moment, the deal they'd made settling heavy on their shoulders. Tasha lingered behind, her eyes on Marcus, caught somewhere between doubt and respect. "If we end up on the news," she said, "I'm blaming you."

Marcus grinned. "Long as you spell my name right."

The hallway surged with bodies, lockers slamming and voices bouncing off the walls like a heartbeat gone wild. Marcus broke off for history class, Darnell headed toward the gym, still clowning about whether the Bunny Man rocked Nikes or Timbs. Tasha slipped into another wing, spine stiff but eyes sharp, clocking everything. Andre slowed his pace to match Jasmine's, close enough to stand with her, far enough to let her breathe.

Jasmine hesitated at the threshold of her classroom, fingers brushing the cool metal of the doorknob. She glanced back at Andre, her eyes searching his for reassurance. "What if they're still out there?" she asked, voice brittle.

Andre gave a hard look, no confusion in his face. "Then we run," he said flat. "And if we can't... we beat they ass."

Jasmine let out a quick laugh, light and gone before it even bounced off the walls. "For real? You think that's gonna cut it?"

Andre considered, then nodded. "For tonight, it'll have to be."

"Boy you crazy," she said with a faint smile, turning to walk into the classroom.

"I gotta be, to go along with Mar–Mar's crazy idea," he said to her as she disappeared into the room.

Andre turned toward his own classroom, a gnawing doubt creeping into his mind. Would "together" really be enough to face whatever waited for them?

****

Fourth-period History dragged on inside a cinderblock box, the walls heavy with the ghosts of generations who'd already suffered through it. Dust and chalk hung in the weak sunlight leaking through the blinds, coating everything like a slow-spreading rash. The desks sat in rigid rows, scarred with initials and crude sketches, each year's crop of students carving proof they'd once been trapped here too.

In room 224 Mr. Johnson pinched a nub of chalk between his fingers and dragged a crooked underline beneath yesterday's half-erased scrawl: Baltimore—Industry—1940s-80s. The chalk squealed, and a few students winced.

He turned, the fluorescents hummed overhead, but his voice cut through it clean.

"Baltimore's factories," he said, scanning the rows, "no only made steel and ships. They made neighborhoods. They made families. They made the city breathe."

A strip of sunlight leaked through the bent blinds, laying bars of light across the desks. Dust drifted in the beam, catching on the carved initials and crude sketches that scarred the wood.

"Who can tell me," he asked, eyes darting from face to face, "what happened when those jobs started disappearing?"

Silence. A cough in the back.

Mr. Johnson leaned forward, glasses sliding down his nose, gaze sharp enough to pin the room in place. "Don't tell me you forgot already. Friday wasn't that long ago."

A girl near the window shifted in her seat and raised her hand halfway. "Didn't people... start leaving the city?"

His mouth pulled up a little, like a grin trying to sneak out. "Exactly. And what happens to a city when the work leaves before the people do?"

The question hung there, heavier than the dust in the light.

He focused on the students, before placing the piece of chalk down.

"Come on, somebody knows," he pressed, eyes flicking from face to face. "What really went down when those jobs started disappearing?"

The usual silence. A cough. A yawn so cavernous it threatened to dislodge the ceiling tiles.

Mar-Mar, who had never met a dare he didn't like and never missed an opportunity to goad the teachers, felt himself leaning forward. He'd spent most of his academic career playing the edges of attention, never fully invested, always running some private commentary in his head. But this morning his focus had shifted and became interested in the topic.

Mr. Johnson's eyes found him. "Mr. Anderson, you look awake for once. Want to help us out?"

Marcus shrugged, easy with it. "You talkin' 'bout the mattress spot, right? The old joint by the tracks? If that's what you mean—business shut down, everybody outta work, whole hood falls to shit. My bad...I mean gets worse. Straight lose-lose."

A low ripple ran through the class—someone muttered "creep city," someone else snorted—but Marcus ignored them, eyes locked on the teacher.

"I would agree to all of that! Not the cursing, the rest of it," Mr. Johnson beamed, as if a secret had been shared between them. "The ACME Mattress Works. A Baltimore original." He turned and paced before the blackboard, words flying from his mouth like iron filings from a magnet.

"Now, you kids might see that building and think it's another dead factory, another piece of urban rot. But at its peak, ACME supplied mattresses to every hospital and hotel from here to New York. Employed nearly five hundred people—" and killed a bunch, too," said a girl near the window, never bothering to look up from her phone.

A few snickers. Mr. Johnson's mouth twitched, half a smile and half a grimace.

"True, true. There were accidents. Manufacturing was a dangerous job, especially back then." He rolled a piece of chalk between his fingers, tiny dust motes drifting down. "But there was pride, too. My father worked the loading dock. He used to say you could smell fresh canvas from a block away—"

"That place smells like piss now," said a boy in a Baltimore

Ravens hoodie, stretching his legs into the aisle.

Mr. Johnson didn't flinch. "Most things do, eventually. The point is, it mattered to people. Gave them a purpose. When the plant shut down in '86, it was like cutting a vein for this side of town. Some folks never really recovered."

The clock above the door ticked with arthritic slowness. The windows buzzed with the memory of last night's rain. Outside, a couple of old heads played basketball in Easterwood Park.

Mr. Johnson's gaze swept the room, checking for comprehension and finding mostly boredom. "Any questions before we move on?"

This time Mar-Mar didn't wait for the silence to gather. He raised his hand, arm rigid, voice firmer than he intended. "What about the dude who got murdered there? Back in the day. Like, for real, not some made-up ghost, the Bunny Man."

The air shifted. Phones lowered, pens stilled. Even the radiator took a moment to hush.

Mr. Johnson's smile faltered, but only for a moment. "Ah, the legend persists," he said, as if it were a mosquito he could simply wave away.

"Everyone around the way know that shit ain't bout nothing," another student said in the back of the classroom.

"That body they found on the tracks ain't saying that," Mar-Mar continued.

"First, watch your language in my class Kelvin. Second, I heard about that on news, but the sad thing is, they may not be the last," Mr. Johnson said.

"So, the Bunny Man, is he real or not," Mar-Mar pressed.

"Well, the guy is real, the legend not so much. The guy would be Clarence Brown. Railroad engineer, if I recall. He helped maintain the rails used to ship out materials. Lot of mystery around his death, but I'm afraid the truth is less exciting than the stories you hear," Mr. Johnson explained.

He leaned back on the edge of his desk, legs crossed at the ankle. "What do you know about it, Mr. Anderson?"

Mar-Mar shrugged again, but the movement felt different, like a shield instead of a joke. "Exactly what people say. That he got caught stealing copper and they... you know. Made an example of him. Some folks say he still haunts the place."

A moment passed where no one breathed.

"Well, you can always count on teenagers to make things interesting," Mr. Johnson said, but the bravado had leaked out of him, replaced by something closer to pity. "The real story is a sad one. According to what we really know, Brown was a good man—worked overtime, kept his head down. Maybe he did see something he shouldn't have. Maybe he was in the wrong place at the wrong time. Either way, the company hushed it up quick. The union, too." His eyes flicked to the window, as if expecting the ghost of Clarence Brown to materialize in the parking lot.

Mar-Mar pressed on, hunger for detail growing teeth inside him. "But they never found out who did it?"

"Not officially," the teacher said. "There were rumors, accusations, but the investigation fizzled. You know how it is with people who work the margins. Easy to forget, easy to lose." His hands gestured vaguely, erasing invisible names from a ledger.

The clock ticked again. The heat pulsed. Mar-Mar felt his skin prickling, as if the story had crawled off the page and into his blood.

Other students had tuned out—the girl with the phone now painting her nails with correction fluid, the boy in the hoodie drooping over his desk like a molted birds' nest. But Mar-Mar's attention sharpened with every word, the details assembling themselves in his mind: the battered body in the shadow of the loading dock, the hush money, the whispered threats that never made it past the foreman's office. He could see it, almost, a sepia film unspooling behind his eyes.

The next slide was supposed to be about city zoning ordinances, but the word "Bunny Man" had detonated in the air and nothing else could grow in its radioactive shadow.

Mar-Mar had meant the question as a kind of test—a way to see if the old stories still had power, or if Mr. Johnson was another teacher on autopilot, bleeding through the same tired notes. But as soon as the word left his lips, he saw the transformation in the man behind the desk. The teacher's posture slackened, the animation draining from his face and pooling in the furrows of his brow.

The classroom reacted the way crowds do at a car crash: some drawn in, others sickened, none willing to look away for long. The girl with the whiteout set down her pen. The boy in the Ravens hoodie sat up, pupils dilating. Even the usually bulletproof indifference of the back row melted into uneasy attention.

Mr. Johnson set his glasses on the desk and rubbed the space between his eyes, as if the memory hurt. When he spoke again, his voice was pitched low, a confession meant for the living but haunted by the dead.

"They called him the Bunny Man because of his hat. Stormy Kromer, with earflaps. Looked like rabbit ears if the light hit right." He looked up, scanning the faces for a trace of recognition. "But there was nothing funny about it. Nothing cute."

A deep quiet gripped the room.

"He worked the midnight shift. Liked the solitude, I think, or maybe it was the only slot left for someone like him." Mr. Johnson paused, waiting for someone to ask what "someone like him" meant, but no one took the bait. "Clarence Brown. He lived two blocks from here. Had a wife, Beatrice, and a little girl who died before she could walk. Not much else."

Mar-Mar's mouth was dry, the taste of chalk dust lining his tongue. He felt a weird kinship with the man in the story—someone who never quite fit the world's expectations, someone who kept moving while the ground threatened to swallow him whole.

"The way I heard it, there was a problem with the union. Not enough work, too many mouths. Folks started getting desperate. Tools went missing, copper walked off at night. People pointed fingers." He hesitated. "In those days, it was easy to blame the guy who didn't talk much. Or the guy whose skin wasn't the right shade for the neighborhood."

A boy in the back muttered something about "typical," but Mr. Johnson ignored it.

"One night, they cornered him by the loading docks. Said they wanted to ask him some questions. But people get braver in the dark, don't they?" Mr. Johnson smiled, but the curve of his lips was a wound. "Nobody ever admitted to what happened. The official report called it 'a random disappearance.' But his wife knew better. She heard the screams from their window. The whole block did."

He picked up a piece of chalk and drew a quick outline on the board—a stick figure in a hat, Xs for eyes. "After that, people said they saw him at the factory, or on the tracks at night. Always in the hat. Sometimes with blood on his hands, sometimes with nothing but silence. My father told me once that if you lived near the tracks and heard tapping on your window after midnight, it meant Clarence was looking for company. I'm pretty sure the whole thing was a way to keep kids from wanting to go onto the tracks."

A girl near the radiator pulled her sleeves over her hands. The windows, unwashed since autumn, sweated.

Mar-Mar felt a pressure behind his eyes, as if every detail of the story pressed itself into his skull like a thumbprint. He wanted to ask why nobody did anything, why nobody told the truth, but the words wouldn't form. Instead, he watched the teacher's hand as it hovered near the stick figure.

The class shifted in their seats, trying to look bored. A couple of laughs slipped out, brittle and quick, dying before they reached the back row. Most kept their eyes fixed on the chalkboard, or above Mr. Johnson's head, faces blank, like they were somewhere else entirely, someplace they didn't want to be.

Mr. Johnson clapped the chalk from his hands, the noise sharp as bone. "History's not only names and dates," he said. "It's the stories we keep telling, whether we want to or not." His eyes lingered on Mar-Mar, dark and hollow. "The past is never gone, no matter how hard you try to bury it."

He turned away and shuffled his notes, but the next slide—zoning codes and building permits—fell into a black hole where no one could hear it scream. The rest of the class period passed in a trance, the air heavy with the scent of old sweat and ghost stories.

When the last of the slides flickered away and the overhead bulbs guttered back to life, the classroom felt like a mausoleum where the bodies had yet to be moved. There was a silence so deep it pressurized the air, squeezing the oxygen from every set of lungs.

Mr. Johnson stood motionless, knuckles white against the edge of the metal desk. No one moved, not even Mar-Mar, who had never before in his life hesitated to break a silence. The teacher's gaze crept across the classroom—over the not-quite-disguised fear, the shame, the sudden hunger for an explanation that would make the story just a story again.

He exhaled, the sound ragged. "They never found him," he said. "Clarence Brown. Not all of him, anyway." His fingers wandered over a tattered city map pinned beside the blackboard. The old Bentalou neighborhood was highlighted in faded orange, the mattress factory a blackened thumbprint at the corner of two angry red lines.

"They say the men who did it hid him in the rocks under the tracks. Some think he's still there, part of the city now." He tapped the map, nails clicking in a slow, deliberate rhythm. "Every generation tries to dig it up. Every generation fails. But who knows for sure, for all we know, he could have left town and never looked back."

For a moment, the class was lost in the image: a body fused to a building, a grudge embalmed in brick and rust, a city gnawing forever on its own gristle.

"Yet, with either theory, it's not something we talk about in the open," Mr. Johnson continued, voice splintered. "The police didn't care. The company was said to have paid off the families. It was easier that way." He looked at Mar-Mar—no longer as a student, but as an inheritor. "But the pain doesn't leave. It finds new shapes. New people."

He turned to the class, searching for a foothold. "There's one person left who remembers. Mrs. Beatrice Brown. Lives by the underpass, only a few blocks away from ACME. She never moved on. Never wanted to."

The bell's shriek was a mercy, a rupture that gave the living an excuse to flee the dead. Chairs scraped, bags zipped, but for a few seconds nobody stood, as if the spell needed time to unwind.

Eventually once everyone realized that school had officially ended, a stampede erupted, students eager to escape the gravity of the lesson. Mar-Mar lingered behind, staring at the stick figure on the board, the rabbit ears drooping like broken wings.

"Mar-Mar, you hitting the court tonight?" one of his friends called out, clapping a hand on his shoulder as they strolled by, snapping him from his thoughts.

"Not sure, I might. I have a few things to handle," he answered, as he stood and gathered his things in a fog. He watched the rest of the class slither out the door, their bravado curdled into unease. The story had stuck to them; he could see it in the way they hunched their shoulders, the way they darted glances at the empty windows.

At the threshold, he felt the teacher's hand on his shoulder. The grip was firmer than expected, but not unkind.

"Listen," Mr. Johnson said, voice pitched for him alone. "You want to know the truth? Don't look for it in books or police reports. The city forgets on purpose. But the people who were left behind—they remember. Some things never stop hurting."

Mar-Mar nodded, unsure if he was supposed to feel grateful or condemned. His head buzzed with the legend, the map, the name of Mrs. Beatrice Brown. He walked out into the corridor with the ghost of Clarence Brown pacing a few steps behind him, a phantom of bad history and worse intentions.

The rumor, he knew, would mutate again. By next class session it would be about haunted tunnels and flesh-eating rabbits. But tonight, it would be a dare, a destination. But for Mar-Mar, it had already become something heavier. A dare not to be afraid, but to finally understand why.

He touched the outline in his notebook—two Xs for eyes, the ears drooping—and felt the truth staring back at him, hungry and unfinished.

ACME Dare

The final bell hit like a starter's pistol, and the school let out in a controlled stampede—shoelace strings and shrieking laughter and the musk of deodorant fighting last period's defeat. On the patchy grass outside Carver Vocational Technical High, the five survivors gathered in the shadow of a dying maple. Marcus showed first, wind-muscled and radiant in his game-day hoodie, the kind of leader who'd rather die than let the silence speak.

Darnell arrived in his wake, backpack slung over one shoulder, eating chips from a plastic bag and licking the residue from his fingers as if savoring the end of childhood. Tasha kept to the perimeter, scrolling her phone and giving the world side-eye, while Andre watched everything like he expected the sidewalk to collapse beneath them. Jasmine appeared last, arms cinched tight around her notebook.

"What y'all waiting on, lets do this," Marcus said, and they fell into formation. Darnell's laughter skipped ahead, punctuating the soft drag of Jasmine's steps. The air was thick with spring mud and last night's rain. Cars blared by, old buses snorted at the curb, and in the distance the city waited like a dog on a chain.

The bus stop to the ACME building was five blocks south, down a street lined with vacant lots and chicken carryouts. A group of older heads played dice on the corner. The friends threaded through them, Marcus in front, pulling the others forward with invisible string. Tasha huffed at his urgency. "What's the rush? ACME's not going anywhere."

"Neither are you if you don't pick up those little legs," Darnell snorted, but Jasmine's face showed only a spasm of embarrassment.

At the bus stop, Marcus checked his phone, the horizon, and his phone again. "It's coming," he said. "Y'all ready?"

Andre grunted, "Suppose."

Darnell glanced up and down the road. "You really gonna do the whole haunted tour, Mar?"

Marcus's grin was all teeth. "Just wait."

The city bus hissed to a stop, doors folding open like a wound, and they piled in. The air inside was wet and warm, laced with onion, cologne, and the mineral scent of steel. They took the middle seats—Jasmine and Andre squeezed against the window, Darnell and Tasha across the aisle, Marcus planted in front, his knees braced against the battered seatback.

Outside, the dirt bikes wheelies past: block after block of row-houses, their paint baked to dust, yards littered with mattress skeletons and busted toys. Some houses had their windows gummed over with plywood, some hung flowerpots or flags. Kids swarmed a playground that looked like it was built entirely out of concrete. On one block, an old man stood on a milk crate, preaching to the pigeons.

Several blocks later the bus veered left at Lafayette, Jasmine's eyes tracked the passing world, but her hands never stopped their anxious dance, a metronome for the story that wouldn't die.

The bus groaned to a halt by the old bridge. Marcus stood up, chin high. "This is us," he said.

They filed off, five sets of shoes hitting the cracked sidewalk in imperfect unison. The bus pulled away, its engine coughing black into the evening air.

In the near distance, the ACME Mattress Factory sprawled like a fallen beast, windows smashed out, rusted water tanks perched like tumors on the roof. The friends clustered on the curb, a pack against the emptiness, the story alive and circling above them.

Marcus looked at each of them, eyes bright. "Ready to see a ghost?"

"Slow your role, Mar. We have a few hours before we're hitting that place up," Darnell said.

Tasha exhaled.

Jasmine kept her gaze on the factory, as if it were already looking back.

Andre took her hand in his, "If you keep staring, it might bite back," he laughed as he pulled her along towards the bridge with the others.

Midway over the bridge, the city's noise warped, unraveling like static from a radio dragged past its signal. The group slowed, and stopped as the last orange rays skimmed the top floor of the ACME Mattress Factory, turning every broken window into an eye. The air was motionless, expectant, so even the distant noises—sirens, basketballs dribbling in the playground at the foot of the bridge, a dog barking in the next neighborhood—fell silent.

That's when the thumping began.

Not the slam of a car door or the static of wheels hitting a pothole, but something older, more deliberate: a steady, rhythmic pounding of metal against metal, echoing from deep inside the factory's gut. It rang in the bones. One, two, three, four—pause—then again, each blow dragging out until you felt it before you heard it.

Darnell was the first to break. He spun, eyes wide, every joke burned from his mouth. "Nah, that's not normal," he said. "That's not some wind or cat or—hell no." His words tumbled over themselves, unfinished, every vowel stretched tight with uncertainty.

Marcus leaned over the rail, trying to see past the glare of the setting sun. "Who's there?" he yelled. His voice cracked on the last word, but he masked it with a cough and a scowl.

Tasha shot him a look. "You think the ghost is gonna answer, idiot?"

But she was nervous, too—her fingers twisted the ends of her sleeves, and the phone in her hand trembled with every thump. She took a video, and immediately lowered the phone, as if afraid of what she might catch.

Jasmine leaned into Andre, clutching his arm tight. She didn't say anything, but her breathing went quick, and her nails left little marks in his jacket.

The pounding stopped as suddenly as it had begun. For a few heartbeats, nobody spoke or moved.

Marcus, who is never one to let fear finish the sentence, grinned. "Y'all heard that, right? It's gotta be someone in there. Crackheads be everywhere."

"Or something," Darnell whispered.

"It's probably a squatter," Marcus said, but the thrill in his voice betrayed him. "I bet if we go after dark, we'll see the real deal."

Tasha glared. "You just want to get us killed for a Tik Tok

video. No way."

Marcus squared up to her, voice dropping into the cadence he used when he was selling a play on the field. "Come on, Tee. We're not kids. You said yourself—cops don't know what they're doing. They already combed the place, and they missed whatever did that." He jerked a thumb at the factory, still vibrating with the echo.

"I said it as a joke," Tasha replied. "Nobody actually goes looking for murderers except the police or loved ones of the victim, Marcus."

Andre let his arm go slack in Jasmine's grip, but he didn't move away. "You go if you want," he said, voice flat. "We don't have to follow you."

"Please," Marcus shot back, "like you're gonna let me go in alone?"

Darnell, never able to bear a dare, found his voice. "He's got a point, Dre. If something happens, better to be together." But the confidence faded from his face as soon as he'd said it.

Jasmine's eyes darted from the factory to the ground. "I don't like it," she said. "What if whoever did that—" she gestured toward the police tape—"is still there?"

Marcus shifted tactics, looking at Jasmine with a gentleness that rarely surfaced. "We'll stick close. Nobody splits up, nobody does anything dumb. We simply look, and we leave."

Tasha stared at her phone, glanced up at the sky, calculating. "What if the person in there has a gun, or a needle, or—"

"After that, we bounce," Marcus said. "We're not heroes. But don't you want to know?"

The idea hung there, as sticky as sweat on skin. For a moment, nobody argued.

Jasmine loosened her grip on Andre, but she didn't step away.

"I'll go," she said, voice a whisper, "if everybody goes."

Andre sighed. "Fine. But I lead. And the second something looks off, we leave."

Marcus grinned, victory stretching across his face. "Deal. Tonight at nine. Meet by Red Door. We'll cut through the lot behind the carryout."

Tasha muttered, "You're so dumb," but her lips quirked at the corners.

Darnell tried a joke, but all that came out was, "I hope you can run fast, Mar."

"Better than you," Marcus said.

They started walking, the bridge behind them and the factory already turning to silhouette. The city noise picked up again, life rushing in to cover the wound left by the pounding.

But the sound lingered in their heads, a threat and a promise.

As they reached the foot of the bridge, Marcus slowed, letting the others pass. He looked back at the ACME building, counting the windows, the stories, as if knowing would give insight. The legend felt closer now, almost real enough to touch.

He tapped the rail, once, twice—testing the echo—and hurried to catch up with the group.

****

The city had drained itself of color and purpose by nightfall, leaving only the jagged shapes of its ruins to scrape at the sky. At the intersection of Payson and Mosher, where the old Red Door bar leaked neon from behind barred windows, five silhouettes stitched themselves together against the sidewalk. A sour, rootless wind bled down from the viaduct. Everything else—car horns, distant barking, the pulse of traffic—had abandoned the block to the ghosts and whoever was dumb enough to meet them.

Marcus stood ten paces apart from the group, a figure sculpted out of swagger and impatience. The blue LED of his watch cast spectral light onto his palm. Every few seconds, he'd flick his eyes up the street and back down, as if afraid time itself might make a break for it. The others huddled in the spill from the Red Door sign, their faces pale and blurred, hands sunk deep into the pockets of their hoodies.

Tasha scanned the horizon for evidence while her thumb—already in camera mode—snapped pictures of herself along the empty street. Her voice, when it came, was low and urgent. "You think it's really out here?" she asked, the question floating toward the gutter where rainwater and cigarette butts clotted in the dark.

Andre said nothing. He positioned himself behind Jasmine, a wall with muscle but not malice, and watched the bar's red light carve halos around her hair. Jasmine's arms locked at her sides, her feet pointed slightly inward, like she was bracing for a hit she couldn't see. The shadows pressed against her back, greedy and close.

Darnell shifted from one foot to the other, the nervous energy in his legs working its way up into his mouth. "So, this the part where the music gets all spooky and one of us dies first?" he said. "Because if it is, I got five bucks on Marcus." The joke skittered into silence and died.

Marcus rolled his eyes, but the edge in his voice cut close to the bone. "Why y'all acting scared? We ain't gonna be out all night. In and out, that's it. See what this Bunny Man mess is about, take a selfie, and bounce." His confidence was half armor, half dare as he slowly approached the group.

A passing car—one headlight out, windows taped with trash bags—creeped up the block and turned the corner without slowing. The five of them waited, breaths synced to the doppler shift of the engine until it vanished completely out of sight. Marcus checked his watch again, before he motioned with a tilt of his chin. "Let's roll. If we stand here any longer, somebody's gonna call the cops on us."

"That sounds better than what we're about to do," Jas murmured, but her words hung in the air, unanswered. Whether they heard her or chose to disregard her unease, the silence wrapped around them like a shroud, amplifying the weight of their shared thoughts.

They moved as a knot, Darnell's laugh echoing off the shuttered daycare and the busted mailbox at the curb. The street beyond the bar was a canyon of dead row houses, their stoops cluttered with wet newspaper and cracked planters. Tasha stopped every half-block to snap a photo—streetlights shattered, a fallen security camera, an abandoned stroller tipped sideways on a storm grate. Darnell kept up the monologue, but every punchline trailed off at the edges.

Further along Mosher Street, the group cut across the desolate parking lot that once belonged to a Super Pride Market decades prior. The sign still loomed overhead, its letters mostly intact, the building faired no better, the windows were fogged with decades of neglect. Marcus led, each step a challenge to the asphalt, which repaid him with a crunch of gravel and sand. Behind him, Tasha veered wide, camera flash catching a family of rats as they sprinted for cover beneath the rusted cart corral.

The air changed. Behind the store, the night thickened, as if the city itself were closing a fist around their necks. The streetlights failed completely here; the only illumination came from the faint, red pulse of the bar sign, already distant, and the slivers of moonless sky visible between the telephone wires.

Jasmine lagged, eyes on her feet. Andre noticed and slowed his own pace until they matched. "You good?" he whispered. She nodded, not trusting her voice. Taking her hand, he offered a lopsided smile, and for a moment they shared the feeling of being the only two real people left in the world.

Marcus reached the back fence and waited. The chain-link was choked with weeds, stray plastic, and the wreckage of years of human neglect. But at one end, behind a rotting pallet, the links had been clipped and pulled aside. It made a ragged door, big enough for someone Marcus's size to slip through. He turned to the others, a king at the drawbridge of his ruined kingdom.

"Told y'all," he said. The smile that split his face was equal parts triumph and challenge. "Come on. This is the fastest way to the tracks."

Darnell peered at the gap. "Bro, that's not a door. That's a tetanus trap."

Tasha, unfazed, stepped up and raised her phone to document the opening. She snapped a shot, before she reached out and pulled the fence wider, fingers nimble. "It's fine," she said. "You go first, Mar."

Marcus dipped his head and ducked through, the metal scraping his jacket but leaving him unmarked. Inside the fence, the world felt smaller and meaner. The grass grew in clumps, waist-high in places, and the ground sloped toward a muddy ditch where the runoff from the city gathered in sullen puddles.

He turned, crouched low, and beckoned for the next in line. Tasha slid through with practiced ease. Andre gestured Jasmine ahead, but she hesitated. He gave her a nod and made a show of going first, widening the opening with his shoulder and pushing with his back to clear a safe path for her. Jasmine followed, hands up, careful not to snag anything.

Darnell brought up the rear, but not before pausing to check the street one last time. "Last chance to run y'all," he said, but no one answered.

They huddled together past the thicket of stubborn weeds, at the foot of a gravel path. The city loomed behind them, but beyond its edges, an unsettling hush had settled, swallowing the sounds of the world whole. The train tracks were only a hundred yards ahead, gleaming faintly where the streetlights failed to reach. Beyond them, the ACME Mattress Factory reared up in silhouette, its blacked-out windows stacked like rows of empty teeth.

Marcus started forward, his stride long and confident. The rest followed, bound by the gravity of the dare and the certainty that if they stopped, they'd never start again.

Tasha snapped another photo. Andre kept close to Jasmine. Darnell's jokes had dried up, but he muttered to himself, maybe to keep the fear at bay.

Marcus, leading, looked back once to make sure the others were still behind. He grinned, the moon filled sky reflected in the whites of his eyes.

He didn't slow down, not when the gravel path narrowed, not when the weeds clung to his ankles like hands reaching from a shallow grave.

The police tape still marked its territory, a jaundiced ribbon fluttering from splintered posts and battered sign poles. By the time the group reached it, the wind had whipped it into a banner for the dead—half-shredded, stained in spots where the rain had soaked through something that would never come clean.

The five teens stopped short of the line, shoes crunching to a halt on loose gravel. Marcus was first, but he too hesitated, the familiar script of bravado replaced by a hush. Tasha swept her flashlight across the ground, the beam landing on a wide, irregular stain that fanned out from the ballast like a flower in full, rotted bloom. Bits of bone-white stone and bottle glass glimmered where the blood had dried.

They formed a rough semicircle around the patch, light overlapping and deepening the color from black to something almost alive. Marcus crouched low, his fingertips hovering over the edge of the stain. "That's blood," he whispered, the words thin as breath.

Andre's voice came from over his shoulder, clipped and cold: "No shit, bro." He didn't look at Marcus, but kept his eyes fixed on the stain, jaw working through whatever words he'd left unsaid.

Tasha leaned in with her phone, zooming close for a shot. The flash lit up the rocks, making the blood look new again. For a second, the air smelled faintly coppery, sharp enough to cut through the chemical tang of railroad creosote. She swallowed and took a step back, hand trembling as she checked the gallery for evidence.

Darnell, who'd been narrating their adventure up to this point, suddenly lost his script. He shifted from foot to foot and took an involuntary half-step back from the tape. "Nah, man. That's too much," he muttered, and for once, nobody disagreed.

"Come on, you're acting like this is your first crime scene," Andre remarked, his gaze fixed intently on the grim tableau before them.

"So, what if I have, it's not like I made it a hobby," Darnell said.

Jasmine stared at the stain, frozen in place. Her eyes were wide and wet, and her hands had knotted themselves into the hem of her hoodie. Andre noticed, and without thinking, lean toward her until their shoulders touched. She jumped at the contact and relaxed into it, her breath slowing as she blinked hard against the image.

Somewhere within the factory's decaying embrace, a sound emerged—a harsh metallic scraping, like rebar dragged across the unforgiving concrete floor. It began as a whisper, a mere suggestion in the stillness of the night, but as it ricocheted off the cavernous walls, it sharpened into something ominous. The group froze, hearts pounding, every gaze snapping toward the factory.

Marcus stood, wiping his hands on his jeans as if he'd touched the stain. He looked at the others, the dare still flickering in his eyes, but something else there now, too—maybe regret, maybe curiosity, maybe the knowledge that he'd set something in motion he couldn't call back.

"We came this far," he said, voice hushed and unfamiliar. "Ain't no point turning back now."

Nobody answered. Instead, they waited for someone else to go first. It was Marcus who took the first step toward the factory, slipping around the edge of the police tape like it was a finish line. The others, bound by the gravity of the night and the dare, followed.

Marcus stopped and squinted up at the factory. His bravado fluttered and reassembled itself. "This is it. Place is beat to shit."

A chunk of foam insulation hung from a drainpipe like a decaying tongue. Graffiti wrapped the base of the walls: crowns, devils, a cartoon cop bent over in humiliation. The chain-link fence around the property sagged in places, and weeds poked through the mesh like the fingers of something buried alive.

Tasha's camera caught a sign, half-torn and canted at an angle: NO TRESPASSING. A different hand had scrawled "Don't let him in" in black marker under the warning.

Jasmine caught up and wrapped her arms around herself, eyes darting to the corners of the yard where night pooled thickest. Andre kept close, boots crunching deliberate and slow.

"We going in?" he asked, but Marcus had already found the gap in the fence and was picking his way through.

They filed after him, the building's face watching them, each window a socket hollowed by time and rumor. The stench of mold and scorched rubber grew stronger the closer they got, and every step sent a nervous ripple through the group.

Darnell squeezed through, and spun to check the fence behind, as if expecting it to heal and trap them inside. Andre and Jasmine went last, his hand never leaving her shoulder until they were through.

Tasha lifted her phone once more, but paused, her thumb hovering indecisively above the screen. The atmosphere around them had shifted, thick with unspoken words and a weight that pressed down on her chest. She adjusted the angle to capture a selfie, the others trailing behind her in a blurred line. With a click, she immortalized the moment, five silhouettes elongated and distorted by the flickering glow of the city lights, each shadow a whisper of what lay ahead.

At the base of the loading dock, Marcus halted, and for a moment none of them spoke. The world had compressed into this patch of ground, this building, and the legend waiting inside.

Above them, the empty windows flickered with reflected light before going still. The ACME Mattress Factory waited, and the five friends, one by one, took their places in the story.

The yard beyond the fence was a minefield of debris: spent spray paint cans, the twisted skeleton of a shopping cart, weeds grown monstrous on a diet of dumped trash. The ground sloped up to the loading dock, where a set of busted stairs led to the gaping rear entrance.

They made their way, flashlights jittering with every footstep. The windows above watched in rows, blank and empty, but it was the dark at ground level that seemed to pulse and breathe. Somewhere inside, the scrape sounded again, closer this time.

At the foot of the loading dock, Marcus paused, forcing a grin. "Ready?" he asked, but the word didn't carry the usual charge.

"Just do it, so we can get this over with," Andre said, and there was no challenge in it, only resignation.

Marcus nodded and ascended the steps, each creak echoing like a warning beneath his feet. The others spread out behind him—Tasha veered to the right, her flashlight cutting through the darkness, while Darnell lingered close, his nervous energy palpable. Andre and Jasmine took up positions on the left, their eyes scanning the shadows that stretched and twisted around them.

At the top, the loading dock yawned open, the darkness beyond impenetrable except where their flashlights carved slices through the air. The scrape had stopped, replaced by the hush of breath and the tick of their shoes on old concrete.

Tasha flipped her phone upright, thumb already on record. "Yo, check this," she whispered, angling the camera toward the entrance. The screen caught Marcus shifting from foot to foot, jaw tight like he was ready to bolt. Jasmine hugged her arms across her chest, eyes darting everywhere but the door. Darnell tried to grin, but it came out crooked, his shoulders hunched low.

Tasha whispered into the mic, half-joking, half-serious: "Tell me this don't look like the trailer for a horror movie."

On playback, the video showed them frozen in the doorway, wide-eyed and restless, like they were waiting for something to lunge out of the dark.

Darnell whispered, "This is some straight-up Final Destination shit," but even his voice had lost its shine.

Marcus took a step inside the dock space, and another. The others followed, not because they wanted to, but because there was no other story left for them to tell. Several feet ahead a metal door hung half off its hinges ahead, a black triangle of deeper shadow beneath it. As they neared, the silence thickened, and every heartbeat echoed off the walls.

Marcus paused a yard from the door and turned to look at the others, waiting for permission, or perhaps a final dare.

None came. Instead, Andre stepped forward and, with a quick nod to Jasmine, reached out and nudged the door with his foot.

The scrape rang out again, so loud it drowned the world.

The five of them froze, pressed together on the threshold of the dark, waiting to see which would break first—the door, the night, or themselves.

Behind them, the city had gone silent. Ahead, the factory waited, its secrets stacked deeper than mattresses, ready to smother anyone who came looking.

Into the ACME Abyss

The darkness inside the ACME Mattress Factory was thick enough to drown in. It pressed from every side, swallowing the teenagers' cell phone flashlights in black soup and spitting back only the briefest glints of corroded metal or gouged cement. The air was viscous, sweet with rot and mold, a flavor that slicked the tongue and lingered in the lungs.

Marcus went first, prideful stride already shrinking beneath the weight of a thousand imagined eyes. His sneakers made no sound on the dust-clotted concrete, though the noise in his head—anger, bravado, that old tickle of panic—was a drumline in his skull. His hand, which held the phone, was slightly unsteady; he tried to grip it tighter hoping the others had not noticed. Each time the beam cut a swath through the dark, the shadows gathered out of reach, forming and unforming into hunched shapes with too many limbs.

Darnell was second, walking so close that Marcus could feel the heat of his breath when he whispered. "Yo, this shit is some Saw II type beat." The words were shriveled, not the full-throated jokes of earlier, but Darnell clung to the ritual of humor like a lifeline. Every third step he'd brush up against Marcus's back, using contact as shield and reassurance.

Tasha trailed behind, phone up like she was live-streaming to nobody. She held it close to her mouth, talking low but steady, like she was trying to convince herself she wasn't scared.

"Time check—two seventeen. Smell in here? Nasty. Like sour trash mixed with dead rat or something. Floor's busted, glass everywhere, random fabric scraps all over."

Her light swept slow across the room, catching the ceiling way up high where rusted beams crisscrossed like broken ribs, then dropping down to the maze of dead machines crowding the floor.

"Yeah," she muttered into the mic, "this place feel like it's waiting on us to mess up."

Each time she triggered the flash, it exploded in white against the dark, leaving afterimages pulsing in the others' eyes.

"Damn, Tasha, you trying to blind us or catch a ghost?" Darnell complained, rubbing his face after another burst caught him square.

She smirked, steady. "Aight, you got some genius plan for how I'm supposed to keep track? Lemme hear it. If not, go 'head and shut your eyes, cross your fingers, and pray it works out."

"Or you can just stream it on TikTok," Darnell smirked.

"Yeah, great plan—let's broadcast our little break-in to the world," she replied, her gaze fixed ahead, dismissing him with a wave of her hand.

"Girl, you know he's scared of the dark," Andre called ahead, while Jasmine walked beside him, their hands locked in a grip that made their knuckles pale.

Andre's body seemed larger in the ruin: every muscle tensed, his back hunched and knees bent slightly, ready to pounce or retreat. Jasmine's free hand held her cell as she used it flashlight to illuminate anything ahead. Neither spoke, but their presence—quiet, dense—acted as ballast for the group, anchoring them to a reality beyond myth or rumor.

The first few yards inside the factory were a gauntlet of hazards. Old mattress guts—yellowed foam and burlap—lay strewn like viscera. Smashed fire extinguishers left patches of pink dust underfoot, and hunks of twisted metal poked out from beneath collapsed conveyor belts. Water dripped from somewhere above, forming iron-red puddles that mirrored the moving beams of their lights.

Marcus slowed at a cluster of huge machines, their silhouettes monstrous and animal. "Yo, D.T.," he hissed. "You see that?"

Darnell nodded, face pinched. "That thing looks like it eats people."

Tasha stopped, lifting her phone to capture a long, slow panorama. "Those are press rollers. Used for flattening the mattress layers before stitching."

Marcus stared at her. "You got all that from Google?"

"I read the packet Mr. Johnson gave out," Tasha replied, deadpan. "You should try it sometime."

"Man, I could listen to you geek out all day. Like when you talk nerdy on us," Darnell teased, a hint of a smirk breaking through his tension.

"Shh, just focus and keep searching," she said, redirecting her gaze to the shadows that loomed around them.

They pressed on. The machines grew denser, some toppled on their sides, others held in place by spiderwebs of wiring and conduit. The walls bore murals of graffiti—angry tags, outlines of lewd figures, a single massive rabbit spray-painted in a shade of violet that almost glowed in the dark.

A bit further, a battered control panel rose from the mess, its buttons and levers furred with dust. Marcus's beam lingered on the emergency stop, a bulbous thing the color of a rotten cherry.

He reached out, finger hovering above the surface.

"Don't touch that," Jasmine whispered, eyes darting everywhere at once.

Marcus's hand dropped, but he covered the retreat with a snort. "It ain't even live. Power's off."

"You don't know that," Jasmine replied.

Andre squeezed her hand, not taking his eyes off the shadows. "Jas is right. Leave it."

Tasha kept the phone close, talking low like she was doing some crime-scene podcast. "Yo... it's colder in here. And look— footprints. Sneakers, for real."

She swung her light down, catching the floor. Their own tracks cut messy through the dust, but under them were others, some faded, some sharp as if freshly made.

She sucked her teeth, steadying her voice. "Yeah... somebody else been through here. Not that long ago."

Darnell bent to look, but straightened, posture stiff. "I wonder how old this is?"

"Could be days or years; could be crackheads going in and out," Jasmine murmured, her voice barely above a whisper.

In the main production hall, the space opened up—an acre of nothing, lined on either side with the half-gutted remains of sewing stations and inspection tables. In the middle, a pool of old mattresses towered ceiling-high, some still encased in plastic, others peeled open to reveal fungal blooms and black smears that might have been blood. Crumbling plaster walls exposes twisted, rusted pipes that snake through the structure like the veins of a dying beast.

The group stopped, collectively unwilling to get any closer to the heap, their light beaming in every direction to take in the place.

"Don't like that," Andre murmured.

Tasha snapped a few pictures. "I bet if you set that pile on fire, you could smoke out the whole neighborhood."

"Bro, what if there's something inside?" Darnell ventured. He edged behind Marcus, using the bigger boy as cover. "Like a fox, a dog with rabies."

"Shut up, Darnell," Jasmine said. She said it softly, but her voice was steady now, no longer trembling. "If anything, somebody just need to light this whole spot up and be done with it. Place mad dumb anyway."

Marcus pointed his light at the top of the mattress mound. "We should check it out," he said, half-dare, half-threat.

Tasha's mouth twisted in disgust. "You first, King."

Marcus considered, then shook his head. "Forget that, shits might have bedbugs."

They skirted the mattress pile, careful not to let their lights stray too far from the group. The air was heavier here, each breath catching in the throat. A muffled thump echoed from somewhere deep in the building, distant but definite.

Darnell's eyes shot wide. "Did y'all hear that?"

Andre nodded, slow. "Probably the building settling, rats, who knows."

"That's some big ass rat," he laughed away.

Tasha held up her phone, talking low like she was on live. "Yo... we heard somethin' movin'. Don't know where it's comin' from—probably just the building creakin', but still."

Jasmine's phone vibrated in her pocket, the sound a cruel little jump-scare. She fumbled it out, screen glowing with a text from her mother: "U home?" She typed back "on my way back soon, wrapping things up with friends," the lie souring her tongue.

They moved toward the far wall, where a row of half-shattered windows admitted a few sickly strands of city light. On the windowsill, someone had left a line of burnt-down candles, their wax melted into puddles like the remains of a prayer.

Tasha stopped, phone up by her mouth. "Yo... this lookin' like some ritual type mess. Low-key got that creepy vibe," she muttered into the mic.

Marcus rolled his eyes, but his grip on the flashlight was shaky. "Man, that's the most Scooby-Doo mess I ever heard," he muttered. "But you ain't lyin'... this spot got me mad uneasy."

Jasmine exhaled, "Let's hurry up already.."

They kept moving, steps less hesitant now, eyes starting to wander instead of dart. The dark corners didn't twitch the same way anymore, and the silence felt more like a pause than a threat.

"Man," Darnell said, kicking at a busted spring poking out of a mattress, "these joints still comfier than juvie beds."

A couple of them snorted, one rolled her eyes, but nobody shut him down. If the laughs were weak, they still stuck around this time.

A narrow side corridor opened up, less clogged with debris, and Marcus took the lead through it. The air reeked of mildew and old paint. At the far end, a door sagged wide onto a cramped break room. A round table lay overturned, chairs either splintered or piled against the wall. Across the chalkboard, in looping, childish script, someone had scrawled: No Rest for the Wicked.

On a battered filing cabinet, a half-empty bottle of gin caught the light, its contents sloshing in the gloom. Tasha snapped a photo, "Somebody been party in here," she said.

Andre shrugged. "Homeless guy, probably. Or the clean-up crew."

Jasmine's gaze drifted to a faded photo tacked to the wall. It showed a group of men in a work uniforms, each one standing proud in sure. On their heads Stormy Kromer hats.

"I wonder if one these is him," Jasmine whispered.

"Is who," Andre asked.

"The Bunny Man," she murmured, her voice low and cautious, as if speaking the name might summon the lurking shadow from the depths of the factory.

The others crowded in to look. Each of the men's face were unremarkable and obscured by the photos age: their eyes dark, each sporting a style mustache of the time.

"Any of these can be Clarence Brown, if he's even in it" Tasha read from the photo's caption. "Employees of the month. November 1955."

Marcus stared at the photo, lost for a second. "None of these look like killers."

"And what does a killer look like exactly," Jasmine asked.

"I don't know, you know, angry, crazy-psycho type," he answered.

"But for real, what do you think happened to Clarence Brown?" Tasha asked, stopping her recording and turning to face the group.

"Honestly, I think he was in the wrong place at the wrong time," Tasha said, her voice steady but laced with curiosity. "Maybe he saw something he shouldn't have."

Darnell leaned against the wall, arms crossed. "Or maybe he was a scapegoat. You know how people get when they're scared. They blame whoever closest."

Jasmine nodded, her brow furrowed. "Yeah, like if someone

stole something from the factory, they'd point fingers at him because he didn't fit in. Easy target."

Marcus scoffed, shaking his head. "Nah, I bet he was up to no good himself. I mean, who knows what kind of shady stuff went down back then? Maybe he was stealing from the company and got caught."

Andre raised an eyebrow, challenging Marcus's theory. "But that doesn't explain why they'd go as far as to kill him. That's some serious overkill for theft."

"Maybe it was personal," Jasmine added, her voice barely above a whisper. "What if someone had a grudge against him? Like, he was a worker, but maybe he crossed someone powerful."

"Or maybe he was just a hard worker, trying to make a living, and they wanted to silence him," Tasha added, her tone growing more intense. "It's always the good ones that get caught in the crossfire."

Darnell shook his head, unease written all over his face. "Whatever went down here had to be brutal. Look at it—whole spot stinks of bad vibes. Wouldn't even shock me if ghosts popped out right now."

"Ghosts or not, we need to keep moving," Andre said, glancing at the shadows creeping closer. "This isn't a place I want to spend the rest of the night."

"Right," Marcus agreed, forcing a laugh to mask the tension. "Let's not end up like Clarence. I'm not ready to join the Bunny Man's fan club."

Whispers in the Dark

The stairs up to the ACME factory's second floor had long ago shrugged off their coating of rubber treads. Now every riser was a scraped, naked edge, the wood underneath carved with initials and bruised by the weight of decades of failed ambitions. The handrail, once brass, was so scored and sticky with grease it recoiled under Marcus's grip.

At the landing, Marcus turned to Darnell with a smirk, the whites of his eyes catching the ambient murk. "You scared?" he said, not loud, but it landed heavy. Darnell, two steps behind, made a show of checking his nails and whistled tunelessly through his teeth.

"Not unless you about to fall through the floor, Mar. You break it, you buy it."

But the laugh that followed sounded wrong—stretched, too brittle, and the way it ricocheted off the cinder block walls made both boys pause.

They stood in the corridor that ran the perimeter of the upper floor, lined with glass-fronted offices now blind with grime. Marcus panned his flashlight down the length of it. The beam knifed through dust and found only more doors, each crusted with a layer of the city's slow forgetting. The glass vibrated minutely under the hum of the wind, as if something large and unseen paced the factory's roof.

The air up here was different: still, but so thick it threatened to clot in the lungs. Some rot, some hard-to-place tang of chemical sweet—something like the flavor of leaking antifreeze in the mouth. But underneath all that, a faint metallic tang.

Darnell inhaled through his nose, "Smells like old pennies and ass," he coughed once.

Marcus flashed a quick grin and stepped up to the door marked Supervisor. The knob bit cold against his palm. He twisted, shoulder pressing in, and the frame gave way with a damp, sucking pop—as if the room itself didn't want to be opened.

Inside: a coffin of a room, one long desk against the far wall, the rest filled with gray light and floating particulate. A cork board held up with dull pushpins, its contents long since stripped away. On the floor, a collapsed leather office chair, stuffing bleeding out in yellow clumps through its cracks.

Marcus swept the room once, twice, and moved to the desk. Its surface was scored with rings and knife marks, but beneath the top sheet of dust lay a buried civilization—slips of paper, a warped Polaroid, a pen with no cap.

"Man, I'm telling you, I bet there's money in here," Darnell said. He edged in behind Marcus, the bravado returning in increments, but he kept a wary eye on the interior dark corners.

"Money? What, in Monopoly dollars?" Marcus snorted, but already he was rifling the drawers. The upper one stuck; he yanked, and the entire face came off in his hand. Inside, a slow-moving horror of silverfish scattered, vanishing into the black. He shook the drawer, cursing, and used his phone's light to probe deeper.

"Check it out," Marcus said. He'd found a metal badge, its lettering eroded but still legible: "Night Shift Supervisor—

Authorized Personnel Only." He pinned it to his chest with a flourish, then gave a two-fingered salute. "Guess I'm the boss now."

You wish you were the boss," Darnell quipped, as he was emboldened, tried the next office door. This one opened easy. He swung his light in a lazy circle and found only toppled filing cabinets, drawers yanked open and vomiting ancient folders. He poked at one, and the paper crumbled between his fingers.

"Yo, these look like, I don't know, science fair instructions," Darnell said, holding up a sheaf of technical diagrams. The lines and numbers meant nothing; the annotations were in a kind of shorthand that made his brain itch.

Marcus joined him, picking through the debris. The folders were labeled in block capitals, sometimes strings of letters and numbers: "QC-511," "YARD SHIP 17," "RAIL NIGHT-LOG." Some pages had brownish stains around the edges, as if someone had once tried to make a sandwich with them.

"Bet you five it's about drugs," Marcus said, voice pitched to echo off the window. "Like, this was a whole front. Probably used to ship drugs into the neighborhood."

"Bro, it's a mattress factory. Only drugs in here are for back pain. Or the ones we should be taking for being in here." But even as Darnell tried to laugh it off, he kept glancing over his shoulder at the door. The dark outside the office pulsed, waiting.

Marcus dropped a handful of folders on the floor and made for the far corner, where a gunmetal filing cabinet stood, still upright, its surface corroded to a leprous green. He tugged on the top drawer; nothing. He rocked it back and forth, braced a foot against the base, and yanked hard. This time it screamed open, the sound so sharp and high it set Darnell's teeth on edge.

Inside: rows of folders, their tabs handwritten in a script so small and neat it looked machine-made. Marcus rifled through them at random. "Yo, some of these got names. Brown, C. — that's the Bunny Man, right? Or his government name?"

Darnell leaned in. "He really had a file?"

"Looks like they got files on everybody who ever punched a clock." Marcus pulled one out, and it shed a cloud of dust. The pages inside were dense—pay stubs, incident reports, a yellowing photo ID paper-clipped to the top sheet. He stared at the picture, and back at the badge on his chest. "Man, this is some straight-up horror movie setup. Dude supposedly gets killed at his job, then completely forgotten about."

"Don't start with that," Darnell said, but his voice thinned at the edges.

Marcus dropped the folder back in the drawer, and grabbed another at random. This one was labeled "INTERNAL—INCIDENT." The report inside was brief, barely three lines, but the last sentence had been circled and underlined in red: "Subject found on loading dock, time unknown. No witnesses. See attached." There was no attachment, only a single Polaroid, face down at the back of the drawer.

Marcus flipped it. After all these years, the photo still had power. A shape hunched in the dark, blurred at the edges; behind it, a pair of red glints reflected the camera's flash.

"Tell me that's not creepy as hell," Marcus said, holding it out.

Darnell made a show of squinting, but his hand shook as he reached for it. "Man, that's gotta be a raccoon or a possum. Or maybe a guy with one of those miners' helmets."

"Miner helmet, in a mattress factory—where that even come from?" Marcus let a grin slip back into place, the challenge written clear across his face, though the skin around his eyes pulled tight.

"I don't know, it was the first thing to come to mind, but that beside the point which is, it's creepy as fuck," Darnell continued.

"Well let's see what else is up here before we go back to the others."

The next office was locked. Marcus pressed his shoulder to it, and rammed. The frame gave with a splinter, the door swinging inward. The air inside was colder, rows of shelves lined the walls, each sagging with ledgers and binders. At the far end, a massive desk, untouched by vandalism or the passage of time.

Darnell hesitated, but Marcus motioned him in. "See? Nothing to it."

But Darnell only got three steps before he stopped dead. The surface of the desk had been polished, probably by the last sun to ever see this room, and for a second it reflected their flashlight beams back at them. But it also reflected something else—a movement, fast and silent, that zipped behind them and vanished.

Darnell spun, light up, but the corridor outside was empty. "Did you see that?"

Marcus, caught off guard, laughed loud. "Man, stop. You trying to give me a heart attack?"

But Darnell's hand was white around the flashlight. "I swear, Mar. Something moved."

They both stared into the hallway for a count of three, maybe five, and turned back to the desk. Neither wanted to be the first to open the drawers, so they did it in tandem—one on each side, both with their breath held.

The left drawer yielded only more paper, the smell of old wood and a single packet of saltine crackers gone green. The right: a faded blue ledger, its first page inscribed with a name neither of them recognized. The rest was filled with tiny, obsessive handwriting—long columns of dates, numbers, and the occasional phrase: "Midnight visitor." "Cargo incomplete." "Red hat on third."

"Dude had some issues," Marcus said, flipping through. But the further he went, the less the entries looked like work and the more they looked like a diary. After a while the dates ran together; the final page was the same sentence written over and over, lines growing less legible as they went:

"Still here, still here, still here—"

Darnell closed the book with a snap and stepped away. "We should head back," he said, voice flat.

Marcus started to make a joke, but the words withered. Instead, he nodded, and together they left the office, not quite running, but not taking their time either. Their footsteps echoed behind them, each one a little louder, a little less like themselves.

By the time they reached the stairwell, both were sweating despite the cold. At the landing, Darnell looked back. In the faint light, the glass-fronted offices seemed filled with movement— not people, not anything recognizable, but a restless shifting. Shadows doubled and redoubled, stretching long fingers across the floor.

He shuddered, then caught up with Marcus, who waited, jittering, at the head of the stairs. "Let's get the others," Marcus said, and this time there was no bravado in it, only need.

Together they started down, the dark behind them swelling until it pressed at their backs, urging them faster with every step.

****

On the production floor, sound was a trapped animal. Every step the trio took was repeated back to them from a hundred corners, layered until the original noise was lost. The beams from their phones found the edges of abandoned conveyor belts, tables warped by decades of water leaks, and bins still packed with the shredded foam that once passed for luxury.

Tasha drifted ahead, meticulous in her documentation, pausing every few yards to sweep her phone's camera across the landscape. Sometimes she'd whisper observations into a voice memo app, her language cold and precise as a forensics report.

"Main floor, north side—yeah, somebody lit somethin' up in here," Tasha muttered into her phone. "Burn marks everywhere. Mattress guts all over—don't even look original, probably some fools wildin'."

She dropped low, snapping pics of the charred scraps, and pushed back up quick, shoulders stiff, eyes cutting around the room like she expected something to move.

Jasmine trailed in her wake, shoulders hunched, her own light weaving through the blackness around them. She stuck close to Andre, who flanked her with deliberate nonchalance, but she felt the magnet of Tasha's certainty tugging her forward.

They reached the far wall, where the windows had all blown in, giving the place a view of the train tracks in the city beyond the overgrown foliage. Tasha turned, sweeping her beam upward to a long glassed-in office suspended over the shop floor, its view once meant for foremen and efficiency experts. "I bet that's where they most likely kept the logs," she said, mostly to herself.

"Logs? How do you know this?" Jasmine's voice was a thin

wire.

"My mom loves the History Channel. Shipping records. If there's anything left would be there for sure."

Andre shot Tasha a look, half admiration, half disbelief. "You really think a mattress company keeps secrets worth killing for?"

Tasha shrugged, phone still up. "Man, you never know. Folks done got dropped over way less. Or maybe it's cap, and all we gon' see is some dusty time cards and rat shit."

"I don't get how we shifted from exploring to playing detective," Andre remarked, but Tasha and Jasmine pressed on, their footsteps echoing in the hollow space as if his words had vanished into thin air.

The stairs to the office were steep, the metal treads grated to bare mesh. Jasmine and Tasha stood at the base of the steep stairs, their lights aimed upward, though something was lurking above.

Andre glanced at the pair. "Alright, I'll take the lead," he said, stepping onto the first stair, followed by Jasmine, who kept her eyes on his shoulders, and last wasTasha, who stopped at every landing to note the state of decay.

At the top, the office was colder than the rest of the building, a wind tunnel of broken glass and torn insulation. The main desk faced the floor below, but along one wall stood a battered credenza, its surface slick with dust.

Tasha moved to the desk and started rifling through drawers. "Help me look," she said, and Andre shrugged, then joined her, flipping through warped ledgers and receipts that crumbled in his fingers. Jasmine wandered to the far side of the office, where a row of battered metal file boxes stood guard.

While Tasha did her investigating, Jasmine hovered near the

file boxes, fingers grazing the cold metal. She didn't want to look at the others, or at the night outside, so she let her gaze drift up—where she found a mirror, half as wide as the room, mounted crooked on the wall above the heating vent. Its surface was pitted and cracked, but some segments still reflected.

She felt herself drawn to it, the way a tooth picks at its own cavity. In the reflection, she saw the three of them, rendered grainy and blue by the glass's age. She watched herself tilt her head. Watched herself hesitate.

Behind Jasmine, the dark stirred. A shape uncoiled from the shadows, rising taller than Andre, its frame stretched thin beneath rags that clung like funeral cloth. Atop its head jutted a warped crown of fabric and wire, crooked ears twisting at angles no body should bear.

The face stayed hidden, yet the weight of its gaze pressed against her chest, crushing the breath from her lungs. The air thickened, heavy and sour, as if the room itself had turned against her. Every instinct screamed to run, but her body locked in place, pinned beneath a dread that felt alive.

The room contracted. The mirror rippled, as if dipped in a pool of oil, and for a split second she saw herself flanked by the thing—its hands resting on her shoulders, its teeth too long in a smile meant only for her. Her light flickered and went out. She screamed. She whirled around, heart racing, but found only Tasha and Andre on the far side of the room.

The sound filled the office and overflowed, echoing off the concrete until it lost all meaning. Andre was there instantly, hands on her upper arms, but she twisted away, eyes locked on the mirror.

"Don't—don't touch me," she managed.

Tasha spun, her phone's flashlight a lance in the dark. "What happened?"

Jasmine shook her head, her gaze darting between the mirror and the dim corners of the room, questioning whether it was all a figment of her imagination or if someone lurked in the shadows.

"There was—it was behind me. I saw someone."

Andre turned, squinting at the mirror. "Saw what?"

Jasmine's hands shook so badly she could barely hold her phone. "It looked like a man, but not. The hat, the eyes. It was—" She swallowed, then tried to focus. "It was watching me. Touching me."

Tasha stepped to the mirror, studied it from an angle, before shaking her head. "Nothing here. Probably a trick of the glass, maybe the others shadow."

"It wasn't a trick." Jasmine's voice had gone flat, as if she were narrating someone else's pain.

Andre's gaze swept the walls, shifted to the desk, returned to the mirror. "Jas, it's just the story. The shadows can play tricks."

"Y'all hear yourselves? Talkin' 'bout shadows playin' tricks. Nah—I know what I saw." Jasmine wrapped her arms tight around herself, knuckles pale. "This ain't some story. We not supposed to be in here."

****

Marcus and Darnell heard the scream as a thin, animal note, sucked through the hollowed-out corridors and splintered by the geometry of the walls. The sound traveled with speed, but its meaning landed slower. They exchanged a look—a brief, brittle spark of understanding—and then Marcus was already running, Darnell's sneakers slapping hard behind him.

The stairwell devoured their shouts. Down on the main floor, dust hung in columns, lit by their jerking flashlights. Andre stood at the bottom, a barricade in a battered hoodie, with Jasmine collapsed at his side. She made a sound like a saw working through wet wood—half crying, half trying to breathe. Tasha hovered behind them, voice sharp but failing to stitch the world back together.

Marcus slid to a halt, almost smacking into Andre's arm. "Yo, what's goin' on?" he snapped, all the front gone from his voice.

Andre shook his head, jaw locked so hard his teeth clicked. "She swear she saw somethin' up in that office," he muttered, chin jerking toward the stairs. "In the mirror. I told her it was a shadow, but she ain't buyin' it."

"I keep telling you it wasn't a damn shadow," Jasmine shouted.

Marcus glanced at Jasmine, who stared at her own hands, flexing the fingers as if she couldn't remember what they were for. Darnell knelt next to her, unsure whether to touch her or be near, and settled for being near

Tasha took a step forward, phone's light aimed at the concrete between them. "It was a reflection, Mar. But she says it moved, that it was behind her. I didn't see it, but—" She cut herself off, unwilling to finish the sentence.

Marcus turned to Jasmine. "Jas. You alright? Tell me what you saw."

She kept her eyes down, voice shaky. "It was right behind me. I saw it—in the glass." The words came out broken, like her signal was cutting. "Had somethin' on its head... a hat, ears, I don't even know. Tall. Off. And it smiled at me... but not like people smile. Not at all."

Darnell forced a laugh. "Probably a bum, right? Or maybe your own reflection. Those old mirrors mess with your eyes."

Andre shook his head. "Nah, we was all right there. Ain't see nothin'," he cut in.

Jasmine shook her head so hard her braid came loose. "It touched me. In the reflection, it put its hands on me. I felt it. I did."

Marcus frowned, gaze flicking from Jasmine to Andre to Tasha. His own breath came quick, but he kept his face flat. "You sure?"

"Look for yourself," Jasmine said. "I said what I said."

Marcus hesitated, then looked at Darnell. "Come on. Let's check it out."

The two climbed the stairs toward the office, footsteps echoing in the hollow stairwell. Inside, beams of light cut across the walls, catching on dust and peeling paint. The mirror offered nothing but their own reflections. Marcus planted himself before the glass, studying it. He lifted a hand in a slow wave, forced a grin, teeth flashing back at the room.

"See? Nothing. Old glass, cracks, plays tricks," he said, but his voice was unconvincing even to himself.

Darnell didn't approach. He hovered in the doorway, scanning the corners as if expecting something to lunge. "Maybe the air's bad up here. Maybe it's like, fumes or something."

Marcus wanted to agree. But he remembered the cold on the knob, the way the shadows moved behind the glass. He pocketed the feeling, stuffed it deep, and turned back toward the stairs.

On the landing below, Jasmine was upright now. Andre stood as a silent presence beside her. Tasha paced a small circle, eyes fixed on her phone.

"We should go," Jasmine said, voice stronger than before.

"We're not supposed to be here."

Marcus hesitated, "We haven't finished checking—"

"Checking for what exactly," Jasmine said, cutting his words short. "I was stupid enough to join, that's my bad. But now we have seen the building and should go."

"No one is keeping you Jas, you can leave if you want," Marcus said.

"Man, whatever," Jasmine cut in, already heading back the way they came.

"That wasn't cool Mar," Andre spoke without meeting Marcus's gaze. He didn't need prompting; he followed, shielding her with his bulk.

Darnell shrugged, hands up, and fell in behind. Tasha lingered, waiting for Marcus to make a call.

"Man, fo'real," he muttered, tossing his hands up before trailing after the crew, already a few steps ahead.

The group threaded through the main hall, skirting the mound of mattresses on their way back. Every step set loose a scatter of echoes, each one splintering into smaller sounds that clung to the walls—like the building itself was learning how to speak. Andre's shoulders curled inward, and every few paces his eyes flicked behind, tallying faces against the shadows that trailed them.

Jasmine was almost calm again, the trauma scabbing over. She walked quick, but not panicked, as if afraid that to pause would let the memory catch up to her.

That was when the thumping started.

It was distant at first, barely a rumor, but unmistakable: metal striking metal, the cadence steady as a heartbeat. One, two, three—then a pause—then again, each blow longer than the last, dragging out like a chain pulled over stone.

Marcus froze, hand lifted. "Y'all hear that?"

Nobody joked this time. The sound came from deep inside the factory, the direction they were heading, but it didn't move. It only grew louder, each strike a new scar across the night.

Darnell shot Marcus a wide-eyed look. "Yo... could be some squatter, maybe a fiend lettin' us know this they spot. Either way, we need to dip."

"We're already bouncing," Tasha said, and for once her sarcasm didn't sound like armor.

Jasmine flinched at each hit, but she didn't stop. Andre kept pace as the thumping thickened the air, slowing every step.

They reached the end of the production floor, but the door that led back to the loading dock was now locked. It hadn't been when they came through. A wet streak ran from the base of the door, pooling in a thin line that shimmered even in the anemic light.

Marcus stared at it before turning to Tasha for confirmation of reality. She shook her head, no explanation, no words.

"The doors locked," Darnell said, as he tugged at the handle.

"Boy stop joking all the time," Marcus gripped the door handle, twisting the knob and slamming his shoulder against it, but it remained firmly shut. "Hell is this."

"Like I said, locked."

The thumping kept on, but now it was joined by something else: a low, scraping hiss, as if something dragged itself across the metal rails in the yard.

Jasmine backed away, bumping into Andre. "We woke it up," she whispered. "We shouldn't have come."

Tasha, voice suddenly hollow, said, "Can we go, please?"

"We need to find another way out," Marcus nodded, being sure to stand at the front as they moved back into the building.

The urge to run was massive, but none of them dared—like prey in the open, they kept to a slow, coordinated retreat.

Entering back into the heart of the building, the thumping cut off. The hush that followed was heavier, like the air itself had been nailed shut. It stretched on, thick and waiting, until a new sound bled through—a faint, deliberate tapping. Slow. Measured. It crawled along the walls, circling, multiplying, as if the building had grown fingers and was drumming from every direction at once.

The Hammer Falls

The sound came from the walls at first—a polite, insistent tapping like the heartbeat of the dying. It pressed in, then multiplied, as if every inch of concrete and cinder block in the ACME Mattress Factory wanted to make itself known. Then the sound gathered mass, bled into the floor, and became a pounding so violent it made the old machines shudder and the filaments of dust tremble in the cold air.

Marcus ran first, shoulders squared and eyes darting in every direction, the bravado peeled off by every second of darkness. His flashlight cut ahead in a feverish arc, revealing a corridor that, by his own memory, hadn't existed when they'd entered. Darnell clung to his back like a second shadow, his quips reduced to nothing but short, sucking breaths and the dull thunk of his shoes on wet cement.

Tasha and Jasmine came after, Tasha's phone trembling in her hand as she tried to record the madness while in motion, Jasmine was simply focused on keeping up with the others. Andre brought up the rear, broad and deliberate, one hand out behind Jasmine, the other balled into a fist tight enough to blanch the knuckles. The air burned in his lungs; it was hard to tell if it was the running or the fear that stung more.

The building made no sense. They'd entered on the south side, but the corridors had twisted, split, then doubled back, only to dead-end at freshly plastered walls or doors that looked ancient but were cold and clean to the touch. At every intersection, Marcus would try to orient by memory or by the chemical drift of air from outside, but the cues were gone: each hallway led to another, then another, none ever offering the relief of the exit.

The pounding grew, warping into a rhythm, metal on metal, a hammer falling again and again. The sound seemed to move ahead of them, then behind, then below, until it was impossible to tell if it was coming from inside the factory or from inside their own skulls.

Marcus slowed at a T-junction, barely able to keep the shaking out of his voice. "Which way did we come from?" he gasped, each breath ragged and sharp.

Darnell, breathing hard, pointed left, but the passage there was now bricked over, mortar still wet and the bricks the color of new skin. "It's messing with us, bro," he said, voice hoarse. "Swear to god, it was open a second ago."

Tasha, eyes wide and wild, swept her phone in a trembling arc, recording the corridor in crisp 4K even as her hands shook. "Document everything," she muttered. "Proof. If we get out—if anyone finds the phone—" Her breath stuttered, words unraveling into a threadbare whisper.

Jasmine pressed in close to Andre, hiding by his side. Her flashlight jittered in her fingers. Head up, braid tight along the back of her neck, she muttered under her breath, "We gotta get outta here."

"Keep moving," Andre said, voice tight.

Jogging turned to running—Marcus taking every new path in the vain hope that momentum itself could outrun the logic of the building. Sometimes the corridors squeezed in, the cinder block walls sweating condensation that smeared the light into greasy halos. Sometimes they opened wide, yawning into rooms that looked like they belonged to different centuries, the furniture and debris arranged in little still files of despair: a single mattress, torn open, springs exposed and rusted; a conference table spattered in something that might have once been blood; a row of lockers, all doors open, the metal warped by heat.

They kept expecting to double back on themselves, to see their own footprints or some mark of their passage, but the building devoured all evidence. The echoes of their footfalls were swallowed, returning only when least expected, with the wrong timing, as if mimicking rather than reflecting their noise.

"Yo, anybody got bars?" Marcus's voice cracked. He flashed the phone—no signal. "Dead. We're off the grid."

Tasha checked hers. "Still recording. No signal." She swiped through the camera app, trying to push aside the mounting certainty that the phone itself would betray her soon enough. She muttered a running commentary: "Yo, they funnelin' us! No exits, no way back! This whole place—this can't be real!"

Darnell kept glancing behind, certain he'd see something. "That sound—" he said, "that's a hammer. You hear it, right? Someone's coming."

"Don't," Jasmine whispered. "Don't say it out loud. Just keep moving."

The walls flexed, not physically but in the way they defied the eye's attempt to fix them in place. Sometimes the corridor would lengthen between blinks, stretching until the pinprick of Marcus's light looked a mile away. Sometimes the ceiling would sag with old insulation, hanging like stalactites ready to break off in slabs. Once, as they rounded a corner, Tasha saw a window—a real window, glass intact, the city nightlight fogging the outside. She ran to it, but the closer she got, the smaller it seemed, until it was only a smudge of light on the wall, and then gone entirely.

They passed a door that was open to a room full of sewing machines. The floor was ankle-deep in thread and dust, every step sending up clouds that stuck to their skin in a tacky paste. At the far end, a ragged American flag hung over a chalkboard. In the beam of Andre's light, Jasmine saw that the blackboard had words written on it, repeated over and over in jagged block letters:

"Still here

still here

still here—"

She reached out to touch it, but Andre caught her wrist. "Don't," he said, voice harsh. "Don't touch anything."

They pressed on, the thumping growing louder and more irregular, as if the hammer was now inside their own ribs. The group had stopped speaking, saving their breath for the frantic effort of running. Darnell tripped at a hallway junction, tumbling forward and scraping his palms on the concrete. He looked up, expecting to be mocked, but Marcus yanked him to his feet, not even a joke left in him.

Tasha's phone began to act strange: the screen flickered, then froze, then rebooted, then cycled again. She shook it, whimpering. "No no no no," she whispered, each syllable a little higher, a little more desperate.

In the dark, Jasmine felt her own heart stutter. She thought she saw movement behind them, a flicker of red light or the suggestion of a silhouette, but every time she blinked it was gone. The only certainty was the sound—the hammering, the tap-tap-tap that crept beneath the skin, rising up the spine and lodging itself at the base of her skull.

The corridor choked off at a yellow door, its paint curled like old scabs. Marcus threw his weight into it—metal groaned but held. Andre stepped up, jaw clenched, and drove his shoulder harder, teeth bared with the strain. The door didn't move.

Behind them, the pounding twisted into a shriek, metal dragging over metal, high and hungry. Jasmine flinched. Her arms prickled, breath caught, eyes locked on the dark behind them.

Tasha, shaking now, pressed her phone against the seam of the door, lighting the numbers stenciled above. "I think we're in the offices," she said, words nearly lost to the sound. "But you said they were on the second floor. We didn't go up any stairs."

Darnell, pale and shaking, said, "Doesn't matter. We gotta get away from—"

He stopped mid-sentence as the wall behind them opened like a wound, drywall crumbling to reveal a man-high crawlspace, pitch black inside. Marcus saw it first, then the others: a void in the wall, wide enough for a person, beckoning them forward.

For a second, nobody moved. The hammering stopped, replaced by a silence so thick it made them want to scream.

Marcus found his courage first, grabbing a chunk of splintered two-by-four from the floor and holding it like a club. "Let's go," he said, and ducked inside.

They followed, Tasha shoving her phone in her back pocket, Darnell and Jasmine moving in a huddle, Andre behind. The crawlspace ran straight, then dipped sharply, then opened into a service corridor lined with pipes and cables. The smell was worse here—sweet rot mixed with the acid of corroded metal.

Every surface slick with a film that seemed to slither beneath the light.

They emerged in a new section of the factory, one none of them remembered from the exterior. Here, the walls were raw concrete, the floors sloped and uneven. Marcus took the lead again, limping a little, the makeshift weapon heavy in his grip.

A low grind rolled through the air, deep and seismic, like the building was shifting in its bones. Instinct snapped their heads around, in time to catch the crawl space closing. Bricks slid inward, slow and deliberate, locking into place with surgical finality. The passage vanished. In its place stood a wall, smooth, cold, and absolute.

No one spoke, but the silence said it all: they should've left when they still had the chance.

"Keep moving," Marcus said breaking the silence, but softer now, as if the building might hear.

They walked through the corridor, tripping over old pallets and fallen pipes.

"Yo, think OSHA gonna pull up?" Darnell joked, voice a little too loud, like he was tryna calm them down—or maybe just himself.

"Dammit Darnell, now is not the time," Jasmine snapped, keeping in step with the others.

Darnell took a deep breath in followed suit.

The corridor branched, split, only to rejoin itself in a pattern of loops and dead ends.Twice they circled back to the same collapsed section of duct work. The graffiti shifted each time: first a screaming face, next a spiral, finally a message in fresh blue paint— "RUN."

They did. The sound returned, no longer hammering alone but a chorus of voices—some high, some guttural, all rising and falling together, a song with no melody or sense. The walls shuddered. The light from their cell phones dimmed, flickered, only to brighten once more as they sprinted down the longest corridor yet.

At the end, a single red exit sign glowed above a battered steel door. It was the first familiar thing they'd seen in what felt like hours.

Marcus reached for the handle, but Andre held him back. "Wait," Andre said, voice quiet, "listen."

They all listened. In the hush, Jasmine thought she heard breathing—not theirs, but something larger, slower, patient.

She pressed her ear to the door. On the other side, nothing moved. No wind, no sound at all.

Tasha shook her head, no longer trusting her own senses. "If this is how it ends, at least we tried," she said, and started recording again, though the phone flickered with each touch.

Marcus tried the door. It opened on the first pull.

They stumbled out onto a new floor, one that looked as if it had been constructed in the moments they spent inside the crawlspace. The layout was wrong, each wall at odds with the last, but the air was different—cold and sharp, no longer thick with mold.

They spread out, desperate for any sign of the outside. Andre scanned the walls for a window, a sign, any clue, but it was blank as a tomb. Tasha darted from corner to corner, phone held up like a shield. Jasmine folded forward, hands gripping her thighs, lungs clawing for air like she'd outrun a fire.

Darnell stood in the middle of the room, trembling. "It's a maze," he said, voice hollow. "It's never gonna let us out."

The others didn't argue. The ACME Mattress Factory had them now, and the only way forward was deeper in.

A fresh wave of pounding started, closer this time. It rattled the pipes overhead and sent a cloud of dust down from the ceiling. The sound was so loud it drowned out their voices.

Marcus looked at the others, his face a mask of sweat and fear. "We run together," he said. "Don't stop. Don't split up. We find a way out, or—" He stopped himself, as the expression on the others face, clearly indicate what he was going to say.

He led, the others close behind, as they plunged deeper into the maze, the light from their phones cutting only inches ahead.

The pounding split the world—until the world itself split open.

They hit the end of the corridor, and in a single, shuddering instant, the concrete yawned wide, swallowing the five into the vast hollow of the old assembly line. The ceiling arched overhead like the rib cage of something dead, the upper windows painted black by decades of neglect.

Floodlights still hung from the rafters, but none were lit. The only illumination came from their trembling flashlights. Along the far wall, ancient conveyor belts sagged beneath the weight of mold-caked mattresses and busted machinery. In the center of the floor, a catwalk crossed over a pit once used for repairs— but now a grave for rust and rot.

Marcus led, but all momentum died the instant he cleared the threshold. He stopped dead, shoulders squared, weapon forgotten at his side. The others slammed to a halt behind him, the sound of their shoes lost in the riot of the pounding.

At first, Jasmine thought her eyes were failing her, that the darkness had finally found a way inside her skull. Then she realized: not absence, but presence. A silhouette, tall and gaunt, cut against the far wall by a slant of moonlight. At its crown, two black flaps jutted up at crooked angles: the hat, the Stormy

Kromer, as the stories said.

The Bunny Man didn't move. He stood like a curse made flesh, locked in place by something older than fear. The air around him pulsed—thick, electric—like rage had weight, pressing against the skin, humming in the bones.

His face was a void beneath the hat, a shadow so deep it swallowed the light whole. The coat hung in tatters, long strips fluttering like dead flags, sleeves shredded to the elbow. His hands were black—caked with grime, streaked with something darker, something dried and old.

In one fist, a sledgehammer: long-handled, pitted, slick with use. In the other, a railroad spike, tip jagged and stained, gleaming like a predator's tooth.

For a time, no one moved. The factory seemed to hold its breath as the pounding stilled, the world narrowed to a single point.

Marcus was the first to break, though it cost him: "Run," he screamed, and the sound shattered the spell. He hurled himself right toward the nearest exit, and the rest scattered with him, fracturing like mercury across the floor.

The Bunny Man's head snapped towards their movement, the hat's ears flopping, and in a blink he was in motion—not running, but gliding, every step stretched out by some impossible math of speed and hate. He barreled straight for Marcus, the sledgehammer dragging sparks across the concrete.

Tasha darted left, careening around a stack of old mattress frames, her phone light flickering in a panic. She kept the lens trained on the apparition, muttering breathless commentary as she ran. "It's real, oh god, it's real, he's here, he's—" The words ran together, trailed off as she ducked behind a toppled shelf.

Andre seized Jasmine by the wrist and yanked her after him, but she was slower, still stunned by the sight. In an instant, defying all sense and structure, the Bunny Man appeared close—too close. The hammer sliced through the air, a brutal arc that missed by inches, the sound of it screaming past their ears so sharp it left a sting. Andre barreled down a side passage, dragging Jasmine, who stumbled over the uneven floor, barely managing to keep hold of her phone.

Darnell, caught dead-center in the kill zone, froze for a heartbeat too long. Next he watched the Bunny Man reappear, suddenly close to Marcus. The sledgehammer lifted, its arc wide and brutal. Before the blow landed, terror surged through him. He dropped flat, chest scraping the ground, and crawled, arms pumping, breath shallow, toward the dark safety of the conveyor belt pit. The concrete bit into his skin, and his hands came away black with filth and something sticky. He did not look back.

The Bunny Man lashed out, striking a metal strut right behind Marcus. The sledgehammer buckled the steel with a single blow, sending shards whistling through the air. Marcus dodged, barely, but a chunk of the frame caught him in the thigh, spinning him off balance. He went down hard, hands outstretched, the makeshift club skittering out of reach. He scrambled after it, eyes never leaving the thing in the hat.

From her hiding spot, Tasha kept the phone trained on the scene, fingers trembling as she zoomed in. The screen flickered. Something shifted.

The Bunny Man turned. No face, just that void beneath the hat, sweeping the room like it could smell fear.

Tasha's breath caught. She slapped a hand over the glow, plunging herself into black. Dropped lower. Held still.

She didn't dare blink. Didn't dare breathe.

"Please, God. Don't let him see me," she thought.

Andre and Jasmine found a service door, locked but weak. Andre threw his shoulder against it, twice, three times. Jasmine's hands shook so badly she almost dropped the phone, but she used it to light his target, eyes wide as she watched the splinters of paint and wood fly with each blow. The pounding of the Bunny Man's hammer echoed through the vast room, mingling with the staccato percussion of Andre's assault. The door creaked until it finally gave. They tumbled through: Jasmine first, Andre slamming it shut behind.

Darnell reached the pit's edge and tumbled in, landing midst a jumbled mess of rusted gears and shattered crates. He pressed himself to the ground, crawling on all fours, straining to hear the sledgehammer's ominous rhythm above. A jagged piece of mattress wire snagged his sleeve, slicing into his skin beneath, but the pain was a distant whisper. When he finally dared to glance up, the Bunny Man had vanished—only a lingering, black shadow stretched across the wall, swirling like dark smoke.

Marcus pushed himself upright, wincing as his weight settled on his injured leg. He lunged toward the stairs leading up to the catwalk, each step a desperate gamble as he skipped rungs, muscles protesting with sharp jolts of pain. Reaching the top, he scanned the cavernous room below: Darnell huddled in the pit, Tasha crouched behind an overturned shelf, and the Bunny Man—a flickering shadow—glided across the concrete, first in one place and then suddenly manifesting in another, eyes searching for new prey in the stillness.

The Bunny Man halted, his head tilting as if attuned to a distant sound. With a sudden, fluid motion, he pivoted toward the pit where Darnell lay hidden. In an instant, he sprang into the air, soaring over the abyss with unnatural agility, landing squarely on the metal grating above. Darnell pressed himself against the cold ground, heart racing, stifling a whimper as the dark figure swept by, mere inches from his face.

On the catwalk, Marcus swayed, the world tilting beneath him. He edged along the railing, scanning for an escape. Ahead, a narrow staircase loomed, leading to another service door. He paused, peering down into the abyss where the Bunny Man crouched, sledgehammer poised, listening intently for Darnell's every movement.

"Jasmine," Marcus breathed, barely a whisper. Her voice echoed from the far corridor, thin, distant, and full of fear.

The Bunny Man straightened, ears flaring, before dissolving into the darkness, swallowed by the labyrinth of rusted machinery.

Tasha's heart raced as she dared a glance from her hiding spot. The assembly line lay deserted, the Bunny Man's presence lingering like a chilling fog that coated every surface in a slick sheen. She bolted forward, leaping over the jagged mattress frames, her gaze locked on a reflective sign that could be away out at the far end. She was oblivious to Marcus perched high on the catwalk, or Darnell clawing his way out of the pit, or where Jasmine and Andre had gone.

But the sign, when she reached it, was nothing—a prop, a painted-on hope. The exit door was welded shut, the handle sheared off. Tasha pounded at it, tears springing hot and silent, but the metal didn't budge. She turned, back to the wall, searching for any sign of the others.

The impossible happened: the lights across the factory flickered, stuttered, and died. In the darkness, only the sound of the dragging hammer remained.

Then, footsteps—heavy, deliberate, returned to the room. The Bunny Man was close.

Tasha scrambled along the wall, hands splayed, desperate for a crack, a vent, a miracle. She turned the camera on herself, face ghost-lit by the screen, and whispered: "If anyone finds this, please—please don't come here. He's real. He's—" The footsteps stopped. A new sound, the scrape of metal on metal, echoed from above.

She looked up. On the catwalk, opposite where Marcus was standing, the Bunny Man appeared, towering over the rail, sledgehammer held in both hands. He did not swing—but watched her from a distance, hat ears twitching in a phantom wind.

Darnell scrambled out of the pit, wincing as he landed on shaky legs. He ducked low, weaving between towering stacks of decaying mattresses. Shadows flickered across Tasha's terrified face as she pressed against the welded door, panic etched in her wide eyes. Without a second thought, he launched himself toward her, heart racing, desperate to reach her side before the darkness closed in.

"Tasha!" he yelled, and she heard, turning as he tackled her behind an overturned crate. The sound of the sledgehammer came a heartbeat later, cleaving the spot where she had stood in two. Concrete erupted in a spray of dust and pain. They crawled, wild-eyed, side by side, until they found a gap between the machinery, a space barely big enough for both.

Darnell pressed a finger to his lips, the weight of Tasha's body pinning him down. They strained to quiet their ragged breaths, each inhale a desperate whisper against the oppressive silence that surrounded them. There, they clung, breathless, listening to the Bunny Man's boots drag back and forth across the ruined floor.

Above, Marcus ran the catwalk, the iron shaking under every step. He made for the service stairs, but the Bunny Man was faster, always faster, always behind. Marcus risked a look back, and in the flicker of his light, saw nothing but that endless, starving shadow.

At the bottom of the stairs, he found the door. Locked.

He hammered it with his fists, once, twice, but the sound was drowned by the specter's own hammer, growing louder, closing in. He fumbled for the makeshift club, fingers slick with sweat, and raised it high.

The Bunny Man glided onto the landing, sledgehammer cocked, silent and unbroken by hesitation. Then he moved. Down the stairs in a blur, towering over Marcus, the hammer already rising.

Marcus swung his makeshift club, muscles firing on instinct. The weapons collided with a bone-deep thud, the shock lancing through his arms. He shoved hard, knocking the blow off course, breath catching in his throat.

No time to think. No time to feel.

He turned and ran.

"Move, now!" he shouted, voice sharp with panic as he spotted Darnell and Tasha crouched beneath the machinery.

They didn't hesitate.

Feet pounding, limbs scrambling, they burst from cover and bolted, racing in the same direction they saw Andre and Jasmine head.

Marcus slammed the door with his fists, panic rising in his throat. "It's us! Open up!" Each hit was a plea, reverberating through the empty corridor as Tasha and Darnell crowded close behind him. "C'mon, open it!" he shouted.

"Marcus?" Andre's voice came muffled, uncertain, from the other side. "Where are the others?"

"We're right here!" Tasha cried, her eyes darting back toward the shadows. "Let us in!"

They heard the scuffle of shoes on concrete, the scrape of metal as Andre slid something heavy out of the way. The door strained, and burst open. Jasmine and Andre pulled them inside, their eyes wide with fear and relief.

"What's happening?" Andre asked, his voice tight, but Jasmine's gaze had already landed on Marcus with an accusatory glare.

"This is your fault!" she yelled, anger and fear bleeding into her voice. "You got us into this!"

Marcus, breathless and laden with guilt, nodded. "I know," he said, urgency rising as the thumping grew louder, like war drums closing in. "But we have to keep moving. There's got to be a way out."

Jasmine hesitated, her anger warring with the cold logic of Marcus's words. The sledgehammer strikes echoed, a relentless countdown that left no time for doubt. She clenched her jaw, and nodded, the movement sharp and resigned. They took off, running as one, a pack of shadows racing through the dark.

"Keep going! Don't stop!" Marcus shouted.

"It's right behind us!" Tasha yelled, "I think its behind us."

But a sudden, lethal movement sliced across their path. The Bunny Man's sledgehammer hurtled out of the shadows end over end, aimed squarely for Darnell.

"D!" Andre screamed, eyes wide with horror.

Darnell jerked sideways, terror snapping through him like a live wire. The hammer screamed past his head, and slammed into the doorframe with a crack that shook the air. The force sent him sprawling. He hit the ground hard, breath knocked loose, the world tilting off-axis as he clawed to get upright. His phone skidded away, spinning until it fetched up under a nearby table. For a moment he saw nothing but pinwheels of pain and the acid-white dazzle behind his eyes.

"Don't stop!" Marcus cried, urgency lacing his voice.

Tasha and Jasmine skidded to a halt, disbelief etched into their faces.

"Darnell!" Tasha called out.

But as they turned, they saw him—the Bunny Man manifesting from a whisp of shadow with his back to them, towering and silent over Darnell.

"Go!" Darnell yelled to the others, the word a raw plea.

Over his shoulder, the Bunny Man fixed his gaze on the group, a silent challenge flickering in his dark eyes as if inviting them to step forward and test their courage. The challenge never came. Instead, the floor groaned as a wall rose out of nowhere. Rusted metal, fractured brick, a jagged barricade erupting between them. It cleaved the corridor with brutal finality, sealing Darnell alone with the specter.

With the others out of the picture, the Bunny Man's gaze twisted toward Darnell like a crack forming in reality—slow, silent, and wrong—until the world felt too thin to hold him. The specter gripped the sledgehammer with one hand and effortlessly wrenched it free from the splintered wood, as his other hand held a railroad spike.

Darnell tried to scream, but only a thin hiss left his lips. He crab-walked backward, heels and palms scraping the concrete, but the apparition advanced with deliberate, predator's grace. Every step the ghost took remained slow, nearly savory.

The hammer arced down, missing Darnell's skull by an inch

and shattering the floor instead, sending up a blizzard of fragments. The shock wave reverberated through the floor, and for one stunned second everything stopped: the hammer frozen, the shadow above him haloed in grit and broken light, the ghost's face a bottomless void.

Darnell hurled himself to the side, arms shielding his head as the hammer crashed down again, splintering the concrete beneath him. Pain shot through his forearm, as the sharp grit went soring and tore into his skin like a thousand tiny teeth. A scream clawed its way out of his throat, raw and desperate. This was no mere echo of fear—this was the sound of life unraveling, a soul fraying in a forsaken place where the living had long since turned their backs.

He pushed himself up, adrenaline surging through him like fire, and sprinted down the corridor toward the nearest exit. Behind him, the sledgehammer swung again; he ducked in time, feeling the rush of air as it sliced past, obliterating a cinder block into dust. The Bunny Man didn't chase—he glided, each step unnaturally long, the burden of vengeance evident in the way he wielded the hammer like an extension of his own twisted will.

Darnell squeezed through a jagged hole in the wall, the rough edges tearing at his jacket and skin. Pain was a distant thought. He risked a glance back, heart hammering as the Bunny Man stopped at the opening, motionless, studying him like prey. The weight of that dark gaze bore down on him, stretching time into an agonizing eternity. Then, with an unsettling calm, the Bunny Man turned away, retreating back into the shadows.

Ahead, the space sloped and twisted, narrowing until he had to turn sideways to squeeze through. He ran in blind bursts, hands out, until the next room opened around him—some kind of shipping bay, packed with empty pallets and the stench of ammonia.

He could hear the others now, their voices floating in from the dark. Marcus's bark, clipped and desperate. Tasha's shrill, unhinged laughter—she was laughing now, not because anything was funny but because the only alternative was to scream. Andre's rumble, the wordless sound he made when he was afraid and didn't want anyone to know. Jasmine's was the last: her words ripping into Marcus for being a coward and leaving Darnell behind.

Darnell turned left. Left again. Crashed through a sheet of plastic hung like a curtain. The void ahead stretched wide and black, and needing a moment to breathe, to gather himself, he dropped low and slid beneath a wide conveyor belt tucked slightly in the corner. The world fell into a silence so deep it felt staged, and for the first time in ages, his voice abandoned him.

All he needed to know was the warehouse lay empty, and he didn't dare peek from beneath. No sign of the hat, the coat, the red-eyed promise of his death. Only silence, and the after-image of the hammer hanging, mid-blow, in his mind.

Muted Screams

It felt like an eternity since Darnell had wriggled free from beneath the rusted conveyor belt, and now he wandered through the desolate building, lost and alone. Echoes of his friends' voices had taunted him, but each time he turned a corner, hope surged only to be crushed by the sight of yet another dark, vacant hallway. With the adrenaline fading, the sting of every scrape and cut he'd sustained during his frantic escape from the Bunny Man began to throb painfully. He bit his lip to keep from screaming and concentrated on finding the others.

Behind him, the echo of the sledgehammer forever lingered. In front, the only sound was his own ragged breaths, sawing up and down the corridor. The world was reduced to his eyes constantly panning, scanning the darkness for the slightest hint of movement. He tried to track down the others voice. Yet doing so, took what little energy he had and gave nothing back as their voices faded further and further away.

He paused for a moment, leaning against the door, his forehead pressing against the peeling paint. With a mix of curiosity and boredom, he twisted the knob, feeling the cool metal bite into his palm. It turned with a loose, anticlimactic click, and the door sagged inward, as if embarrassed to put up any fight.

Inside: a short hall, carpet chewed away to the subfloor, water-stained tiles bowing overhead. There were doors on both sides—one with a wire-mesh window that glared at him like an angry cat, the other hung with a sign so faded it might once have spelled out some warning. The light in here wasn't right: it flickered at a rate that made his brain stutter, so that every time he blinked the world seemed to have moved on without him.

He stepped inside, each movement a struggle against the fatigue weighing down his limbs, and as he ventured deeper, the door slammed shut. The click was final, like the seal on a coffin. His hands shook, either from pinching pain or the wet animal fear that had infected his bones. He straightened himself up and prepared for what could come his way. He looked for something—anything—to use as a weapon.

The first door yielded only a closet filled with ancient mop buckets and the dis articulated pieces of a mannequin—legs, a head with one glass eye, a torso scored with deep knife cuts. Darnell recoiled, slammed the door shut, fighting a rising nausea that was as much psychic as it was physical.

He could feel the ACME building breathing. It was subtle at first—the walls flexing, the air pressure shifting, the floor sinking half an inch as if waiting for him to notice. But once noticed, it couldn't be UN-felt. The entire place was a lung, and he was a bacterial invader, to be spat out or destroyed.

He tried the next door, which gave way with a sigh. It opened onto a vast office, the kind with rows of modular furniture stretching into infinite darkness. All the cubicles had been smashed, the particleboard dividers upended or impaled on each other, creating a jagged jungle of splinters and fabric. The only way forward was a tight, crooked aisle between the wreckage.

Darnell hesitated. Somewhere in the maze ahead, a fluorescent fixture buzzed with a predatory whine, oscillating between full blast and strobe effect. Every few seconds, the room blazed like noon, collapsed into black, and drifted into a gray limbo. Shadows moved with each cycle, never resolving into shapes he could trust.

"Oh, hell no," he murmured to himself, glancing back to find an abyss yawning behind him. "Fuck."

He stepped in. The carpet was wet in places, sticky in others. It smelled old. Worse than someone's grandmother's house. The ceiling tiles dripped, but in a way that made him suspect the water was coming from somewhere inside the building's guts and not from any honest rain.

Halfway down the aisle, he paused and tried to catch his breath. His lungs stuttered, greedy for oxygen that felt both too thin and too heavy. His mouth was dry, tongue stuck to his teeth, and when he tried to swallow he got only the taste of stale air.

He called out, "Mar—!" but the word snapped in half and fell to the floor. The walls soaked up the sound, refusing to let even the echo escape. He tried again, voice breaking into a whisper. "Tasha? Dre?"

Silence enveloped him like a shroud. The lights flickered out, plunging him into a suffocating blackness. In that fleeting moment, a presence brushed past him, chilling the air like a spectral hand gliding over his skin. Darnell whirled around, losing his balance as he stumbled against the jagged edge of a shattered cubicle wall. His heart raced, pounding in his ears. When the lights blazed back to life, the office lay unchanged— an indifferent expanse of chaos, yet the air crackled with an unseen menace that twisted his gut.

He kept moving. At the end of the row, he found a collapsed reception desk and crawled over it, wincing as a loose staple tore through his palm. He squeezed his hand, watched the blood well up and drop onto the laminate surface, where it spread with a hunger he recognized.

The next stretch of corridor was impossibly long, each turn a copy of the one before. He moved faster, driven by a terror that something was herding him, funneling him deeper and deeper into the building's digestive tract.

Ahead, the hall ended at a metal door. Upon reaching it, the knob oozed a steady stream of water, as if it were weeping from some unseen wound. He didn't want to touch it, but he was out of options. He gripped the handle, it felt warm and somehow twisted. The door yawned open, spilling him into another office. It was a wide, open space, lit from above by a single, half-dead tube.

At the center of the room was a mound of old mattresses, stacked at crazy angles, some still in their plastic sheaths, others slit open to show the black, crumbling guts inside. Darnell stared, then decided there had to be another way. He turned, to go back, but the door was gone. Replaced by a seamless cinder block wall.

His heart kicked up, went double-time. He tried to call out again, but his voice was a whisper. He edged around the pile, looking for an exit, but the only way out that he could see was a narrow chute between two toppled filing cabinets. He didn't like it, but staying there was not an option.

He squeezed inside and crawled on hands and knees, the space stretching endlessly ahead. The pain in his palms and arm faded, eclipsed by a numb certainty—he wasn't getting out. For a moment, he stopped, breath hitching, the urge to sob rising with a quiet, crushing sense of defeat. The carpet reeked of God knows what, but that didn't matter. He considered lying down, letting the building finish what it started. It would be easier.

Then the wall beside him gave way, crumbling to reveal a short crawlspace where an electronic blue light glowed. He focused on it as a beacon, until he popped out into a tiny room that was barely big enough to stand. There was no exit here, only the blue light, which came from a screen on the desk: a security monitor, cracked but still alive.

A splintered wooden chair stood before the desk. Darnell hesitated, body aching, mind urging him to run. Fatigue pulled at him, tempting surrender, and for a breath, the Bunny Man's presence seemed to lift.

He sank into the chair and stared at the monitor—five small feeds flickering. In one, Marcus, Tasha, Andre, and Jasmine circled the same broken stairwell, trapped in a loop.

"It's pointless," he whispered, hoping the others could feel the truth in his voice.

In the fifth window, a view of the room he now sat in. Nothing moved—until Darnell watched his own battered body crawl into frame, mirrored on the screen, seconds behind his own movement.

He stared at the screen, at himself, at the way his image glitched and shuddered, pixelating into fragments. For a moment he wasn't sure which was the real Darnell—himself, or the one on the monitor.

He pressed his head to the desk and let tears come, waiting for the next round of torment to begin. In the darkness of the room he was in, something else moved. The screen flickered, static snow tumbling over the image. Darnell looked up in time to see it. A long, thin shape crowned with a grotesque hat. It walked slow towards his image in the grainy blue of the monitor, before it lean down, reaching for him.

He spun, but the space was empty.

He blinked, certain that the apparition was merely a trick of his frayed nerves or the building's cruel manipulation of his senses.

But then, in the flicker of the security screen, he saw it again—closer this time, so close the shadow of the hat stretched all the way across the room and into the crawlspace behind him.

He had seconds, maybe less.

He pushed away from the desk and slipped back into the chute that now consisted of collapsed cubicles. With what strength he was able to gain doing his brief respite, he pushed himself, creating space between him in it.

His pants snagged something sharp, splitting open a fresh wound, blood streamed down his leg. Gritting through the pain, he crawled to a rusted vent and smashed it with he palm of his hand. Dust burst into the air, choking him, but he kept going. The second hit echoed even louder.

He slumped in the tunnel, pain blooming through every limb. Dust and sweat smeared into his eyes as he wiped his face. Wincing in annoyance, the world went silent, then immediately fractured. A sound—low, guttural, too deep for a human throat—rolled down the tunnel at him. It vibrated in his ribs.

He froze. The monitor's glow was only feet away, but was also swallowed by the dark. Slowly, carefully, he turned and looked over his shoulder. In the black, the shape he had seen in the monitor had coalesced into the same tall and thin figure. The hat was unmistakable, the Stormy Kromer silhouette cut hard against the blue light.

The face beneath was void. No features, not even the suggestion of a mouth or eyes, but Darnell felt them anyway—eyes like nails, driving into him.

He tried to scream, but the sound failed in his throat.

He shoved at the vent again, but it wouldn't give as the tunnel seemed to shrink around him.

The Bunny Man blocked the only exit behind him, his body crouched to look into the narrow space. In its hand was the sledgehammer, held loose and easy.

Darnell felt his bladder let go, but he couldn't move, couldn't even think beyond the single point of terror that had fixed itself in his chest. He squeezed his eyes shut and prayed, not for escape, but for it to be quick.

A voice, grated down the tunnel, so full of hate it felt like a knife in the ear. "Company men," it said. Or maybe it was the thought of him, that made the meaning so clear it didn't need words.

The Bunny Man rose, sledgehammer clenched, and swung with brutal force. Cubicles tore free, crashing in all direction before splintering apart. Metal shrieked, plastic burst, and debris whirled through the room in a storm of wreckage.

In the clamor, Darnell pried his eyes open, chest hammering, the cubicle frames bowing inward until their edges bit into his shoulders. Steel groaned above him, the tunnel narrowing with every breath.

Behind him, the Bunny Man waited, not rushing, but watching, savoring as he smacks away more and more of the tunnel away, slowly revealing his prey.

Darnell clawed at the vent, the rusted edge, easily peeling away his fingernails until it reached his bleeding skin.

He risked a glance back as the Bunny Man knocked aside a

section of the cubicles covering his legs. The last thing he saw was the sledgehammer, raised high and brought back down on him. He screamed, and the sound echoed all the way down the building, through every duct and corridor, until it was swallowed by the silence.

His scream didn't matter. It bounced once, twice, then shriveled and died. The sound in his head was louder—the shattering, pop-and-crack of his own body as the sledgehammer slammed down onto his ankle.

He didn't see it coming; the Bunny Man's arm moved too fast, too accurate. One second the head of the hammer hovered in the dead air, the next it was on him, breaking the bone so clean that for a heartbeat Darnell didn't register what had happened. Then the pain arrived, a wave of white so pure it wiped out the rest of the world. He pushed forward on his good leg, dragging the ruined one behind—a sack of shattered bones, toes twisted and slick. There was nowhere left to run, only the raw torment flooding every nerve.

He dug his nails into the carpet, pulling himself an inch, then another. Every movement sent razors through his calf, and each pull left a new smeared trail of blood behind. The cubicle walls closed in around him, the panels now is less an obstacle and more of a coffin. He whimpered, coughed, spat pinkish saliva onto the dust.

Methodically, the Bunny Man continued to dismantled the maze, tearing cubicle panels away with deliberate, hungry movements, hammering them aside with supernatural power as if they were nothing but packing foam.

Darnell lay there, a rat at the end of a dead end, his vision going red at the edges. He thought of his mother, of his little sister, and of the friends he'd left behind—like Marcus, who would have been braver, or at least louder, in the face of this. He wanted to be angry, but terror was the only thing left.

The sledgehammer struck again, this time higher, catching the meat of his thigh. The pain was different—dull, sinking, like a punch from inside. He couldn't breathe, couldn't scream; there was only the blinding agony and the sound of his own heartbeat.

Hands locked around the mangled stump of his ankle, dragging him from the wreckage. His fingers raked the floor, nails splitting into bloody crescents as he fought to anchor himself. The tunnel spat him out into the open office, where he crashed onto his side, ruined foot twitching. When he looked up, the Bunny Man stood over him—sledgehammer hanging heavy at its side, ragged ears drooping like torn flags. In its other hand, the Bunny Man held a fistful of railroad spikes, old and rusty and each one as long as a knife.

The boot came down on Darnell's hand, bones crunching until his teeth rattled. The Bunny Man sank into a crouch to align a spike, its face swallowed in shadow, featureless and unreadable—yet the air seemed to warp with its grin. Darnell felt it, cold and triumphant, curling around him like a noose, the satisfaction radiating without a single visible smile.

"Please, no. You don't have to do this. I swear I won't come back," Darnell pleaded, his voice trembling as it echoed into the void, swallowed by an impenetrable silence that offered no mercy.

The spike punched clean through his forearm, nailing it to the floor in a jolt that lit every nerve like fire on a live wire. He stared as the hammer lifted, then crashed down, sinking the metal deeper into concrete—so precise it was almost beautiful.

Darnell choked on the words, each one torn out between

ragged breaths and the hammer's blows. "Please—why are you doing this? What did I ever do to you?" His voice cracked, high and broken, the plea spilling out more like a sob than a question.

The Bunny Man remained a silent and grotesque silhouette against the faint light as he worked.

Darnell's chest heaved, eyes darting through the dark for the faintest trace of mercy in the thing looming over him. His voice cracked, spilling out in a frantic rush. "I can help you! You don't have to do this... please, let me go!"

A laugh broke free from the Bunny Man, jagged and hollow, rattling through the metal walls like the tolling of a funeral bell. His words dripped with scorn, each syllable cutting deeper than the spikes: "Help? You're nothing—but another wretch clawing for yourself, no different from the rest." In the blue light of the monitor, the sledgehammer shimmered, its weight pressing down like a sentence already passed.

Darnell strained to free his other arm, but the Bunny Man's grip held fast. The hammer came down, driving another spike above his elbow, tearing through muscle and flesh. Blood burst across the floor, pooling outward as he stared, numb.

In a blur, the Bunny Man drove spikes through both legs, meat and bone giving way in a single brutal stroke. Darnell's vision wavered, the edges of the world blurring as darkness pressed in.

He wanted to scream, but he was so far under the pain now that it seemed pointless.

He closed his eyes, waited for the next blow.

It didn't come.

He opened his eyes. The Bunny Man had stepped back, seemingly to admire its work, head cocked, the ears of the hat flapping softly as it moved.

With tears streaming from his eyes, Darnell's gaze drifted to the ceiling that was bathed in the monitors flickering hue. The world faded, then surged back. He could still hear the Bunny Man, the sound of its breath, the low shuffle of boots he never saw.

He was still alive. The thought was a curse.

He glanced at his arms, at the spikes that pinned him. He tried to move, but nothing happened. His limbs were dead.

"Please, no," Darnell pleaded, his words weak.

The Bunny Man leaned close, face inches from his own. There was a smell—like sewage and mold and old rage. The blank space where its eyes should have been looked at him, and for a moment, Darnell saw his own reflection in the midst of the darkness, small and broken and afraid.

He wished for death, but the Bunny Man wanted him to see. To see that darkness is present and should not be tested.

He waited, and the world closed in.

He faded out, then back in. The pain never left; it just moved, settling in his arms, then in his legs. He tried to move, but the spikes had him, fixed him to the cold lifeless floor.

He could turn his head, barely, and when he did, the room reeled in nauseous arcs.

The Bunny Man was patient. It stood above him, sledgehammer balanced on one shoulder. The blank face watched, studied, the weight of its attention heavier than any pain Darnell had felt so far.

The Bunny Man wasn't finished. He knelt, pressing a fresh spike against Darnell's thigh above the knee, holding it there in dreadful stillness before the hammer fell. The strike split muscle, scraped bone, and drove through with surgical cruelty.

Agony surged up Darnell's spine, bursting behind his eyes until the world went white and sight itself vanished.

The next spike went in above his collarbone, angled so that it missed the artery but pinned him flat to the floor. The hammer came down, slow and heavy, and this time Darnell barely managed a gasp.

Blood pooled beneath him, warm and insistent. He could see it now, spreading from his body, filling the low spots in the concrete's pockets, soaking the legs of a toppled office chair nearby.

Once again the Bunny Man stepped back, inspected the tableau, and cocked its head. It looked satisfied.

Darnell's eyes rolled. He heard things: the drip of his own blood, the creak of the building, the low hum of the exit sign above. But under it all was a sound—impossible but there—a kind of thumping, a heartbeat not his own, pulsing from the concrete.

He realized then that he was still alive because the Bunny Man wanted it. Wanted him to feel every second, every pound of the hammer, every twist of the metal. He was a project, not a person.

The Bunny Man knelt one last time, and with slow, deliberate force, drove a final spike through Darnell's sternum. The pain was a supernova. Darnell's body seized, every nerve firing at once, and for a moment he saw the whole room lit up in a blaze of color and motion.

A gurgled scream erupted from his mouth, and this time the sound traveled. It ran the halls, punched through the silence of the ACME building, echoed up the stairwells and out into the night.

Far down another corridor, the sound reached Marcus, Tasha,

Jasmine, and Andre—a scream torn apart mid-breath, echoing through ducts and steel like something alive. They froze, the air thick with its aftershock, and slowly turned toward one another. Terror hollowed their faces, eyes wide with the same unspoken truth. The silence that followed was heavier than the scream itself, and in it lay the certainty: Darnell was gone, and whatever had taken him was far from done.

The Bunny Man stood still, listening as the last echo bled into silence. Then the sledgehammer spun once in its grip before crashing down across Darnell's face. Light flared white, collapsed into black, and then—nothing.

Satisfied, the Bunny Man dissolved into drifting wisps of shadow, as if the darkness itself reclaimed him.

For a long while, the room held its breath. Only the blood moved, spreading slow and deliberate from beneath Darnell's shattered body, sketching a dark outline on the floor—a shape destined to linger long after memory failed. The screen flickered once, then died.

The Blood-Stained Stairs

Marcus ran as if the concrete might split and swallow him. Behind, Jasmine's sobs, Andre's curses, and Tasha's stumbling steps blurred into a ragged chorus. The ACME Mattress Factory devoured itself, corridors twisting and collapsing in ways that defied even a city built on broken rules.

The four teens sprinted up the winding stairs, each landing twisting back on itself—identical or entirely different from the last. Tasha followed, trailing as always, her phone held out as both talisman and documentation device, its blue glow painting the walls in colors that weren't on any spectrum you'd find at Home Depot.

The stairwell had never been right, but now it dropped the pretense. Flights stretched or collapsed without pattern, railings jutting into black air or folding back like broken bones. The handrail burned, then froze under their grip. Steps flexed as if the stairwell breathed, while the walls blistered into eyes, hands, teeth—watching, reaching, waiting.

"Don't look back," Marcus ordered, his voice a cracked whip in the dark.

Jasmine didn't need to be told—she kept her eyes locked ahead, each step a blind leap of faith as she prayed for a way out. Andre took the stairs two at a time, his hand at the lower of Jasmine's back, urging her to keep moving, as if she might float away if he let go.

Tasha lagged, not for lack of fear, but because she stopped every third step to snap a photo, or to whisper measurements into her phone's mic. "Landing number twelve," she said, not caring if the others heard. "Man, these steps don't line up—landings all twisted. Geometry straight broke. Air's gettin' thick... and, the walls—they movin'?" Her own voice sounded wrong, as if the phone was trying to correct for her accent, flattening the vowels, removing the urgency.

"Tasha, quit with the damn science experiment?" Andre snapped, not bothering to turn around. "We need to get out, not go viral."

Tasha shot back, "Chill? Ain't nothin' think about—unless you want me talkin' about Darnell, huh?"

"Don't start, Tasha," Jasmine cut in, voice sharp. "Darnell ain't got nothin' to do with this right now."

"Man, enough!" Marcus barked from up front, not bothering to turn around. "We ain't got time to tear each other up. Only thing that matters is gettin' outta here."

The words silenced them, their footsteps echoing on the stairs as the phone light dimmed, weak as spotlights in a meat locker. The glow reached only a few feet, shadows doubling or stuttering ahead like scouts. At times Marcus saw four shadows where there should have been three. At others, none at all.

Halfway up the next flight, Andre stopped dead, nearly sending Jasmine over his back.

"Wait," he whispered. The word came back at them three times, echoing up and down the stairwell, but in the wrong order: wait... wait...wait...Wait.

"What the hell?" Jasmine whimpered, her nails digging into

Andre's arm to keep from doubling over.

Andre shook his head, struggling to regain his breath. "It's not real. Just keeps going."

But it was real. The walls pulsed, in and out, a rhythm so deep it rattled the teeth. The air pressure was making Marcus's ears pop, and every time he opened his mouth to say something, the words came out thick and gummy, like his tongue was wrapped in cheesecloth. He wanted to be brave, to be the leader, but the bravado was gone, stripped raw by the sight of Darnell's empty place in the chain. Now he just wanted out.

It did not take the others long to regain their breaths and continued on, while Tasha stayed a bit longer at the landing.

"Thermal shift," she narrated. "Surface is... it's cold, it's—" Her breath clouded in front of her face, visible even in the phone's anemic light.

"Tasha, get moving," Marcus called out.

The stairs climbed. Marcus counted seventeen steps, but when he looked back, there were only four. He forced his legs on, knees buckling on the long flights, locking on the short. The air shifted with a sharp metallic tang that made him dizzy, then soured—mildew, hot rubber, and finally a burst of animal rot that sent Jasmine gagging into her sleeve.

A landing stretched out ahead, impossibly long, like a hotel corridor at three in the morning. The doors set into the walls were all welded shut, some with metal plates, others with thick, black caulk.

"This isn't right. There weren't this many floors. There weren't. How can it keep—" Jasmine words trailed off, unable to complete the thought.

"It's the building," Tasha said. "It's the Bunny Man. It's fucking with us."

Andre grunted. "It's just an old building. They built it like this on purpose. To keep people out."

But he didn't believe it. Not after what they'd seen on the main floor. Not after the Darnell.

A new sound joined the stairwell's chorus—the tick of metal on metal, like a wrench being tapped against a pipe. It started far below, then leaped up a flight, then another, moving with impossible speed.

Jasmine's shriek ripped through the stairwell, bouncing off the confined space. The others froze mid-step. Their phone lights jittered, shadows sliding together until one black shape sprawled across the wall.

"Yo—what the hell was that?" Andre hissed, clutching the rail.

"Don't—don't look at it," Jasmine stammered, her hand still clamped over her mouth.

Tasha's voice cracked, sharp with panic. "It's us. It's just us, right? Tell me that's just us."

Marcus said nothing. Every instinct screamed at him to look away, but he couldn't. His eyes locked on the wall, on the single shadow that didn't belong. Their lights cut across it, but the darkness held—unyielding, alive. Then he saw them: two red eyes burning through the black. A figure took shape, tall, impossibly tall, its silhouette stretching higher than any of them could stand.

"The Bunny Man," he almost called out, but the words caught in his throat. Instead, he turned and shoved Andre. "Go!" he hissed. "Don't stop for anything!"

The group broke into a run, Andre pulling Jasmine along, Tasha slamming the phone into her back pocket so she could use both hands. The stairs flexed, steps bending as the landing stretched with every stride. Marcus's calves cramped, lungs burned, but fear drove him on like a machine.

Behind them, the tapping grew. They reached the next landing, a wide, cold expanse lit only by a single wall mounted bulb. For a second, the group hesitated.

"Which way?" Jasmine gasped.

Andre shrugged, "Up. Always up."

"This is impossible, the building does not have this many floors," Tasha said as she leaned over, hands on knees, panting. Her phone buzzed with a new alert, a shrill digital whine. She fumbled it out, only to see that every photo she'd taken was gone, replaced by black squares and fragments of static.

"Nah, nah, nah..." she muttered, thumb flying across the screen. "This can't be real. No way."

"What is it," Marcus asked.

"They gone... all of 'em... gone," Tasha muttered, thumb frozen on the last video. Her hand flew to her mouth, eyes wide, locked on the screen. The others crowded in, faces lit by the glow, waiting to see what she couldn't even say.

On the screen, a glitching loop of Darnell played—his face warped, mouth locked in a silent scream, the image tearing and twitching as if the video itself was alive.

Marcus saw it. "What the hell—?" he started, but was interrupted by a new sound: not the tapping, but a deep, wet grunt, as if the building was clearing its throat.

The stairs behind them bent, folding in on themselves, the risers creaking like old bones. The eyes were gone, but the threat remained, pressing up from below.

Jasmine pointed. "There! Another door!" The door at the top of the landing was different from the others, not welded shut but hanging half-off its hinges, as if someone—or something—

had tried to force its way through from the other side.

Marcus didn't wait. He shoved Andre and Jasmine ahead, then followed, Tasha keeping pace.

Inside: another stairwell, but this one was even worse, twisting like a spiral, with steps that grew narrower as they climbed. The group squeezed together, shoulder to shoulder, breathing each other's panic. The walls were a tapestry of peeling paint.

Tasha spoke again, softer this time, "We're being funneled." She shone her phone at the wall, where a thin trickle of red—maybe rust, maybe not—ran in a jagged line from floor to ceiling.

Marcus didn't bother to look. He kept his gaze on the top of the stairs, willing the world to make sense.

It didn't.

At the next landing, the stairwell opened into a small room, barely bigger than a closet. A single, round window overlooked the city, but instead of light, it showed only black—no street-lamps, no moon, just a dense, ink-colored nothing.

Jasmine darted to the window, her fists pounding against the cold glass. "Help! Someone, please!" Panic laced her voice as she pressed her forehead against the surface, pleading for it to shatter and let them escape.

Marcus joined her, slamming his elbow against the glass, each impact sending a jarring tremor through his arm. The cold surface resisted, mocking them, refusing to yield.

"Stop it," Andre chimed in, his voice trembling, "It's not going to let us go. I say we should stay here. Barricade the door."

Marcus shook his head. "It'll just find us. We have to keep moving."

Jasmine huddled in the corner, staring at the window. "It's not outside. There's nothing outside. We're not even—" She stopped, started again. "We're not anywhere."

Tasha pulled out her phone one last time. The screen was dead. She pressed the power button, then pressed it again. Nothing.

Marcus watched her, then looked to Andre, then back down the stairs. "Whatever it is, it's coming," he said. "And we're not going to be here when it gets here."

They left the room, with the stairs looping again, down this time, or maybe sideways. The orientation meant nothing. The only thing that mattered was that they kept moving, kept putting distance between themselves and the thing that hunted them.

The tapping faded for a minute, replaced by the sound of their own shoes, their own breath, the thud of blood in their ears.

Then, ahead, a voice—Tasha's voice—echoed up the stairwell, but she hadn't spoken. It was her own voice, but flattened, re-played, warped. "Landing number twelve," it repeated. "Steps between landings: unpredictable. Geometry not Euclidean. Air pressure rising. The walls are... moving?" Over and over, as if the stairwell itself was trying to memorize the sound.

Marcus felt his guts twist. He stopped, stared at the others, only to find them steadily moving, exhaustion written on their faces.

Andre nodded. "It's copying us. It's—"

Then as if on cue, the stairwell flexed, and reality with it.

One second, Tasha trailed the others, her own breath drowning out their voices. Next, she lurched forward as the stairs stretched, then buckled, the entire landing shifting like a tectonic plate. Andre's hoodie slipped from view around a blind corner, the sounds of Marcus and Jasmine evaporating as if the air had turned to wet velvet. For a moment, she was weightless, drifting above the steps, her body un-tethered from gravity.

She found her footing just in time to smack both palms against a wall that hadn't been there before. The stairwell lights flickered and died, leaving only the shaky glow of her phone, which had mysteriously powered back on. She spun — Marcus, Andre, and Jasmine were gone. Nothing but the endless spiral of steps, twisted and wrong, the landings now stacked at impossible angles.

"Where y'all at," she called out, but her voice was swallowed by the dark.

Staggering forward, she reached a crumbling platform above a caged elevator shaft. Its door hung crooked, one hinge snapped, the other twisted into a rusted grin. The floor quaked beneath her sneakers, and she hugged the wall, fearing her weight might collapse the stairwell into the void.

Behind her, the silence was total — so total that even the sound of her own heartbeat felt like an intrusion. Then the silence changed. The familiar and unwelcome dragging of a hammer along the floor. Slow at first and deliberate.

It sounded like it came from everywhere, but also from within her. She twisted, shining her phone in all directions, squinting into the gloom.

"Marcus? Jasmine? Dre?" she yelled with a whisper.

The Bunny Man stood a dozen steps above her, hunched and long, as if he'd always been there, waiting. The Stormy Kromer hat was crushed down tight, the ear flaps sagging at the edges. He wore the same filthy, ancient coat, but now it was shredded at the wrists, revealing hands so black with grime they absorbed the light from her phone. One hand clutched a railroad spike, the other held nothing, fingers splayed and twitching as if remembering a tool lost long ago.

He stared at her with a face that was only shadow, but Tasha felt the attention like a needle sliding under her skin. He remained nearly motionless, and methodically tapped the spike against a pipe, a ritual, each ring of metal setting her teeth on edge. She wanted to move, to run, to scream for Marcus and the others, but she couldn't find her voice or her feet, all the fear that she ever had was locked onto the shadowy figure.

The Bunny Man stepped down a tread, his motion unsettlingly smooth, like an eel gliding through black water. Tasha shrank back, but the stair behind her was gone, the landing already erased. The only way out was down, and down meant toward the thing in the hat.

She inhaled slowly, trying to steady herself, but her nerves clung tight, unrelenting. The spike's tap echoed louder now, ricocheting off the narrow walls, syncing with the ragged rhythm of her breath.

The Bunny Man glided another step closer, and Tasha caught the shimmer of the spike's old point. His other hand—now, both hands now—reached for the railing, fingers spidering across the cold metal, the nails cracked and caked with something brown.

"Please," she whispered, and hated herself for it.

The Bunny Man stopped, the hat tilting in a parody of curiosity.

Tasha pressed herself to the wall, her phone held out like a crucifix. "You don't have to—" she started, but the words withered.

The Bunny Man smiled. She couldn't see it, but she knew. The darkness under the hat grew deeper, the shape of the jaw shifting as if something inside was pushing to get out.

He stepped off the stairwell and onto the wall, as easily as a bug skittering sideways. For a moment, he was vertical, spike in hand, staring at her. Then he flowed down, landing in front of her with a softness that made her stomach revolt.

He was close enough to touch, if she'd dared. She didn't.

The Bunny Man leaned in, the brim of his hat so near her nose she could smell oil and exhaust. He raised the spike, slow and with a purpose, then drew the tip down the wall beside her, scoring a line in the old, chipped paint. The sound was nothing, not even a whisper, but it might as well have been thunder.

Tasha whimpered, eyes locked on the spike, waiting for the pain.

It didn't come. Not yet.

The Bunny Man slid back, spike held parallel to the ground, as if inviting her to move first.

She didn't wait for a better chance. She bolted sideways, skirting the edge of the platform, and made a move for the stairs below. The Bunny Man followed, but not fast; his movements were measured, patient, like a cat who knew the mouse had no way out.

She ran, barely seeing where she was going, just away down, into the guts of the building.

But the tapping resumed, keeping pace with her, always just a breath behind.

Tasha flew down the stairs, barely touching the last riser before slamming into the fire door—hard. Her shoulder screamed. Her teeth clacked. Stars burst behind her eyes. She clawed at the crash bar, yanking, shoving, cursing—but it wouldn't budge. Rust? Logic? Didn't matter. The tapping was back. Closer. Louder. Mocking. She wasn't getting out.

The phone slipped from her grip, but she snatched it mid-fall, fumbling it to camera mode without thinking. If this was it, if she was about to die, then someone was going to see. Someone had to. She raised the phone, both hands shaking, and braced herself for whatever came.

The Bunny Man appeared at the top of the stairs. For a second, his silhouette blurred at the edges. The railroad spike dangled from his right hand, tapping the metal railing with a slow, tick-tick-tick that seemed to set the lights flickering in rhythm.

She aimed the phone, hands trembling so hard the screen shimmied. "Fuck. Please. God," she gasped, the words spilling out, absurd from someone who never prayed.

He descended the stairs with the spike's metallic cadence keeping pace. Tasha kept filming, thumbed the volume up, desperate for any sound that could drown out the horror. The camera app tried to focus, but the image warped, stretched, snapped back in jagged frames. Each time the Bunny Man's face came into shot, the pixels smeared, turning his head into a void.

She hit record.

The Bunny Man stared at the phone, then at her, and then—between one breath and the next—he was gone.

Not vanished, but erased. The space he'd occupied was empty, and the vary air where he'd stood seemed warped.

The phone's screen lagged behind, holding onto his image for one beat too long, then releasing it in a flare of static that wiped out the last five seconds of footage. Tasha's hands shook, her brain lagging just as bad, unable to process what had happened.

She pivoted, half-expecting him to have circled around, but the stairwell was empty. A laugh escaped her—a high, fractured sound, more relief than joy. She took a step backward, away from the stairs, hugging her phone to her chest.

"Not today," she muttered. "Not—"

Her words were cut short, replaced with a scream which ripped the air, jagged and primal, as white-hot pain detonated in her leg. She collapsed, clawing at the wall for balance, lungs heaving, eyes wide and wild. The spike jutted from her thigh, denim torn like paper around the wound. For a heartbeat she couldn't believe it—couldn't accept it—then the agony surged again, swallowing her whole, dragging her into a suffocating black tide.

Another blow struck, this time the right knee. She didn't see the spike swing, but it punched clean through the joint, the head of the spike blooming out the other side in a spray of bone and blood.

She went down hard, knees slamming against the concrete, hands instinctively clutching at the wounds. The Bunny Man materialized out of the darkness, bending low, his ruined face inches from her own.

He watched as she bled, his eyes flat and hungry. He raised a hand, not with the spike this time, but with his bare palm, and laid it gentle against her cheek. The fingers were cold, the nails chipped and jagged, but the touch was almost careful.

Tasha wept, not from pain now but from the horror of being seen—really seen—by the thing that had lived behind the stories.

The Bunny Man leaned in closer, and whispered something too soft for the phone to capture. The only word she caught was "tragedies should be remembered," the words were rough and hoarse. Then again disappeared from sight.

****

On the fortieth or maybe four-hundredth landing, Marcus stopped to catch his breath and realized the staircase was wrong. Not just the steps, which had stretched and warped like pulled taffy, but the sound—the footsteps behind them had gone silent.

He turned, expecting to see Tasha two paces back, recording or muttering or just being stubborn, but she wasn't there. The air where she should have been was just empty, a hollow patch of nothing.

"Yo, Tasha?" Marcus shouted, hoping for an echo, even a bad one. The only reply was a distant, wet gurgle, and then silence.

Andre doubled back, his face slick with sweat, hands white-knuckled on the railing. "She was just here. Just—" He cut off, as if his voice had been intercepted.

Jasmine glance over the side of the stairwell, eyes rimmed with red. She'd been quiet for a while now, only speaking when absolutely necessary. Now, she pointed: "Down there."

They leaned over the railing as one, and for a moment the vertigo almost pitched Marcus into the abyss. The stairwell spiraled down, landing after landing, each one lit by a single, sickly bulb. On the lowest visible landing, a figure sprawled on the concrete, its limbs wrong, bent in too many places.

At first, Marcus didn't register the blood. It was too much, and too far away, and his brain didn't want to process the contorted form. But then the body twitched—once, then twice, a series of small, mechanical convulsions.

It was Tasha.

"Jesus Christ," Andre muttered, the words leaking out in a whisper.

A high, animal shriek split the air. It started as a sob and ended as a scream, one that Marcus was sure didn't belong to a person anymore. He felt it vibrate in his chest, the kind of sound that rewires a person, makes them different after. He gripped the railing hard, as if it would brace his emotions.

On the landing below, Tasha convulsed violently, as if some unseen hand had seized her and yanked her to a sitting position. Blood streamed from her knees, pooling on the concrete like spilled ink, while crimson leaked from the jagged wound in her thigh, painting the floor below. Her palms slapped against the surface slick with her blood, fingers splayed wide in a desperate attempt to push herself up, but the concrete felt alive beneath her, resisting her every movement.

Marcus watched in horror as she struggled, her mouth moving in frantic silence, lips forming words that never reached his ears—a thin, wet rasp escaping instead, like the last breath of a drowning creature. Each heave of agony she bellowed sent fresh waves of pain coursing through her, and the blood continued to flow. An invisible force twisted her limbs, jerking her body unnaturally, making her look like a marionette with tangled strings. Her head pulled back, one elbow and arm twisted in the opposite direction, eyes wide with terror, reflecting the flickering light above as if pleading for salvation. But there was none to be found. The shadows coiled around her.

Every movement she made felt agonizingly slow, each inch gained a struggle against the oppressive grip of the unseen. A shudder rippled through her body, and she fell forward, only to be pulled back upright again, as if caught in a cruel game.

The Bunny Man stepped into view, not out of the stairs but out of the wall itself, like an oil stain bleeding through old paint. He stood over Tasha, one hand on her shoulder, the other holding a spike.

"No," Jasmine yelled, her voice breaking. She started for the steps, but Marcus grabbed her by the wrist. "Let me go!" she tried again, pulling against his hold, tears slipping down her cheeks.

Andre edged along the landing, looking for a way to get down faster. The stairs here were warped, twisted almost vertical, but Andre was ready to jump, to slide, to do anything.

Back at Tasha, the Bunny Man leaned in. He whispered something into Tasha's ear—Marcus saw the girl's head turn, saw the shock and terror in her wide, rolling eyes. He raised her carefully, until her shoulders hit the wall. Then the spike found her gut. The sound was soft, obscene—fabric tearing, breath breaking. Her eyes rolled, shock and pain locking her in place as he pinned her there like a specimen.

Her body bucked, legs flailing, but the Bunny Man only stepped back. Calmly he lifted the spike and drove it home. The sound was wrong, a rupture that seemed to echo forever. She sagged against the wall, blood spilling in narrow rivers that followed the grooves downward, as though the building itself were bleeding her out.

She was still alive. Her head snapped up, and for a second Marcus thought she was looking straight at him. Her mouth worked, shaping words he couldn't hear.

"Tasha!" Jasmine screamed. The sound bounced off the walls, came back in weird, broken pieces. Tasha didn't react, maybe she couldn't, maybe the pain was too much, or maybe the Bunny Man had already broken her inside and out.

Andre moved to jump the rail, but Marcus locked his arms around him. "You can't help her!" he hissed, voice harsh, almost cruel.

"She's dying!" Andre's face twisted, his voice a howl of agony.

"No! Don't go—don't you get it? You'll die too."

Andre struggled, but Jasmine joined Marcus, all three tangled together at the rail, not fighting, just holding on to each other so they didn't get swept away by the horror.

On the landing below, the Bunny Man stepped back. He admired his work, cocking his head to one side, the ears of the hat drooping over the ruined face. The phone at her feet pulsed like a heartbeat, first once, then again, then went out, but not before her eyes found the three of them.

Her mouth fumbled for words, but only a dry rasp escaped before her body dropped still. Blood seeped out, slow and steady, pooling wide until it shone back at her like a red moon no night should ever hold.

The Bunny Man's head lifted, eyes climbing the stairwell until they locked on Marcus. Distance meant nothing; the gaze hit him like frost in his lungs. Then the figure dissolved, darkness peeling off him in tendrils, leaving nothing behind.

The three of them, Marcus, Andre, Jasmine, stood there, holding on to each other, the sound of Tasha's dying gasp bouncing around the stairwell, fading slowly.

The silence that followed was so absolute, Marcus was sure he'd gone deaf. But then he heard it: the faintest tick...tick...tick, somewhere below, or above, or everywhere at once.

No Way Out

Marcus, Jasmine, and Andre each felt more isolated than ever. The building's insides kept shifting, rewriting themselves in real time, and that did nothing to steady their fraying psyches. At the next corner, Marcus and Andre skidded to a halt. Jasmine didn't. Her foot caught on a slab of loose plaster—then gravity took her. She slammed into the concrete, knees scraping raw against the dust-caked floor. No scream. Just collapse. She folded in on herself, arms shielding her head, body trembling in quiet, broken pulses like something short-circuiting.

Andre reached for her, hand halfway out like he wasn't sure she'd take it.

"Dre, get her up! We gotta move!" Marcus snapped, eyes darting.

"Chill out, Mar. Running ain't doing jack," Andre shot back, not realizing Jasmine hadn't grabbed his hand.

"So what—you tryna post up here and die?"

Jasmine ignored them both. She pressed her face deeper into the crook of her elbow, hair slick and knotted with sweat. The world shrank to black behind her eyelids, but even there she could see it—Tasha's red fountain blooming on the stairs, Darnell's face when the hammer found him. The memories looped and bled, louder than any threat the building could throw.

Jasmine clamped her mouth shut, refusing the tears, until her shoulders... gave up. She sobbed dry, body wracked, the sound so thin it never even reached her own ears.

They were in one of the many corridors, the building had created around them. Though wide open, the air was cold and damp. The floor was a graveyard—crumbled plaster, mouse droppings, and scattered wooden crates, half-collapsed in rotting stacks. Their lids bore faded stencils, codes so old the paint had bled into fungal bruises, marking whatever ACME had abandoned when it closed.

Marcus stepped to the nearest window, boots crunching over a graveyard of dead flies piled thick along the sill and floor. Wings curled. Legs tangled. More casualties. The building had claimed them too—quiet, mindless, and just as trapped. Undeterred, he ran his hands along the seam of the window. It rattled but wouldn't give. "Shit," he said, and kicked at the glass, heel bouncing off as if it were steel. "Dre, help me."

Andre threw his hands up as if saying, *"Man, whatever,"* letting the moment slide off him like it didn't matter—even though it did.

Together, they attacked the window, fists and elbows pounding until their knuckles ached, but the glass didn't even crack. Each impact vibrated down the wall, a tuning fork for the whole building.

Jasmine sat up slow, blinking like she'd just come out of a blackout. Her limbs felt wrong, like somebody else's blood was dragging through her veins, thick and overheated. She wiped at her face, smearing dirt and tears into a gritty paste across her cheek. Her eyes locked on the phone lying face-up on the floor. The battery was gasping, screen twitching between a frozen shot of Darnell's face and static, like it couldn't decide if he was still real.

"It's not breaking. Nothing in this building makes sense. We're not supposed to get out, it's pointless," Andre added.

Marcus turned, jaw clenched so tight it looked carved from stone. "We can't just give up. Darnell—" His voice buckled, snapped shut. He tried again. "Tasha—" but the name choked out halfway, swallowed by whatever was clawing at his throat.

He didn't finish. Just grabbed a splintered two-by-four from the rubble, gripped it like a weapon. "Stay close," he muttered, eyes scanning the dark. "If that thing comes back—"

His words were cut off as the silence that had followed them for so long suddenly shivered, like a tape rewinding.First a static, high-pitched, at the edge of hearing. Then a low scrape, metal on stone, growing in volume until it was impossible to tell from which direction it came. Jasmine reached for her phone, clutched its light like a lifeline, and scooted herself backwards until her spine pressed flat against the nearest wall.

The dust in the hall swirled, agitated by some breath of air. Marcus shined his phone light up and down the hall, but the beam barely made it out; the darkness in the corridor seemed thicker, greedy for all illumination.

Then the Bunny Man appeared, not walking but simply there, like a bad dream snapped into existence. He stood at the threshold, this time abnormally tall that his hat nearly touched the ceiling. His coat—once a rail man pride—had rotted into streamers, and each time he moved it shed a blizzard of black fibers onto the floor. They each took in his negative, blank face where features should be, but his eyes—hollow, sunken, filled with nothing—found Jasmine first sitting on the floor.

He raised the sledgehammer with both hands, the motion slow and deliberate. The head of it was stained, not simply with the residue of old murder but with the fresh memory of the night. The hammer's shadow slithered down the length of the hall, dragging behind it a trail of cold that made Jasmine's bones rattle inside her skin.

Andre broke first. Giving his best war-cry, a sound so high it nearly bent the air, and then charged. Marcus followed a half-beat later, swinging the two-by-four at the specter's head. The Bunny Man did not duck. He let the board hit him square in the hat, and in response, backhanded Marcus with the shaft of the sledgehammer. The impact hurled Marcus backward, his body crashing against the concrete. He skidded along the floor, tumbling multiple times before finally coming to a halt, dazed and disoriented.

Andre threw everything he had—fist to the gut, knuckles to the jaw. The Bunny Man didn't flinch. Didn't blink. It was like hitting a statue carved from nightmares.

Andre managed to grab a fistful of its coat, but the thing moved fast—inhuman fast. Its hand clamped around his wrist, grip like steel forged in hell. Andre was airborne, hurled backward into the same window they'd tried to shatter minutes ago.

He hit hard. Glass didn't break. Just a dull thud, then collapse. His body crumpled in a cloud of dust and dead wings.

The Bunny Man stepped closer. Graveled plaster masked the floor, but his footsteps still echoed—muffled, yet clear, like the sound crawled through the building's bones. He didn't look at Marcus or Andre, not even to check if they would get back up. His gaze locked onto Jasmine. For the first time, she realized—she couldn't move. Not a scream. Not a breath. Fear had frozen her so completely, she hadn't noticed the rusted pipes rising from the floor, curling up on either side like claws. She was boxed in, and the building had done it quietly. She sat, pinned by the weight of his attention, her phone still in her hand, camera light pointed at the figure.

He came within inches of her, the coat's hem brushing her sneaker. The sledgehammer hovered above her and dropped, not to strike but to rest gently atop her bent knees.

He crouched, the movement creaky, almost human. Jasmine stared into the blank, and for a moment she thought she saw herself—tiny and shaking—reflected back, smaller with every second.

"Please," she whispered. "Don't."

He lifted the hammer.

Marcus made a noise, not a word but a sound of pure animal fear. He staggered to his feet, blood leaking from a split above his brow. "Leave her alone," he tried, but it came out slurred, more wish than order.

He lunged with a strike, the two by four inches from the Bunny Man's back—then something unseen slammed into him. No warning. No sound. Only the impact. He flew backward, crashing through the stack of rotten crates, skidding across the dust-choked floor, limbs flailing, until he landed hard several feet away, breath knocked clean out of him.

The apparition never broke eye contact with Jasmine.

Jasmine shut her eyes, hoping for a quick and final blackout.

It didn't come.

Instead, she heard the hammer scrape against the concrete, heard the soft wheeze of the Bunny Man's breath, heard the voice—low, cracked, the voice of every urban legend ever whispered in the dark—say: "Tragedies should be remembered."

The hammer arced up. Slow. As if time itself wanted to watch what happened next.

Andre ran in, reaching for Jasmine, but the Bunny Man's free hand caught him by the neck, lifting him clear off the ground. Andre kicked and clawed, but the grip was inescapable. The apparition's strength was not supernatural, but inevitable, like gravity.

All Andre could do was meet Jasmine's eyes—pleading, drained, barely holding on. The Bunny Man held Andre aloft with one hand, his toes barely grazing the floor. In the other, the hammer hovered, raised, steady, and right above Jasmine's head.

The hammer fell and landed with a sound not meant for living ears. It was a noise both crisp and wet, like a pumpkin splitting under a single blow, but followed by the stickier sounds of bone shattering, tissue giving way, blood atomized into mist. Jasmine's mouth snapped open, but the scream came out silent—a gasp so thin it vanished before it reached the air. The impact jolted her spine all the way to her toes, the force of it driving her body hard into the concrete behind. Her vision whited out, shifted to pink, and sank into a deep, swimming red.

Andre dangled like bait, the Bunny Man's icy grip locked around his throat. He couldn't fight, couldn't move—just hang there and watch it unfold. This time, the motion was not slow or theatrical. The hammer rose and fell in a rhythm, each blow perfectly spaced, each thud followed by a spray of blood that painted the cracked plaster in widening arcs. The sledgehammer caved in Jasmine's face first, flattening her cheek and sending a splatter across the far wall. The next hit smashed her collarbone; the next, her chest. The force drove her body lower each time, until she was a pile of shattered limbs, wet clothing, and broken sounds.

Marcus tried to rise, but his legs failed him. He made it to his knees before the Bunny Man's attention flicked his way. The apparition didn't even pause; it simply kept the hammer going, like it was nailing shut a coffin that could never be made airtight. Marcus's voice finally came back to him.

"NO!" he shouted, over and over, even as the sledgehammer worked its way through Jasmine's body.

The Bunny Man hurled Andre straight into Marcus. Marcus threw up his arms, bracing for impact, but Andre's weight and the force behind it were too much. They crashed together and hit the floor hard, limbs tangled.

Even in the chaos, Marcus found his voice. "We have to go," he said, but it was more a suggestion than an order. He stood and grabbed Andre's arm, and tried to haul him upright. Andre resisted, tried to crawl toward what was left of Jasmine, but Marcus wouldn't let him. He pulled harder, the two of them locked in a dance of pain and panic, until finally Andre's legs remembered how to work, and the pair stumbled along the corridor.

Behind them, the hammer continued its grim work. The rhythm never broke; each strike landed with a consistency that made Marcus want to puke. He didn't look back, but in his mind he saw Jasmine's head split open, the white of bone and the black of brain, her braid tangled with clots and hair and shards of jaw.

Their footsteps tore down the hall, slipping on the blood smeared across the bottom of their shoes. The hallways closed in, every corner tighter than the last, but Marcus kept his grip on Andre, dragging him forward. The only sounds were the slap of sneakers on the floor, their shared panting, and behind them—the wet, endless percussion of the hammer.

They found a stairwell, narrower than any before. Marcus pushed Andre through first and dove in after. The stairs coiled down, up, sideways, as if the building couldn't decide which way to spit them out. They didn't care. Down was good enough. Every landing, Marcus braced himself for the Bunny Man to appear, but the stairwell stayed empty. The violence, it seemed, was content to finish what it started before hunting again.

Halfway down the next flight, Andre collapsed. His knees hit the steps, and he fell face-first, hands scrabbling at the railing for purchase. Marcus tried to help, but Andre wouldn't be moved. He hunched, head in his arms, and let out a sob so deep Marcus thought he might be choking.

"She was right there," Andre said, voice ragged. "She was right fucking there and I—"

Marcus crouched beside him, adrenaline burning out to cold. "It wasn't your fault. You couldn't—nobody could've—" He tried to finish the thought, but he could not bring himself to. He squeezed Andre's shoulder, tried to lend strength.

Above, the hammer had finally stopped it thumps. The silence was total, a zero-point vacuum that sucked every thought out of their skulls.

Andre raised his head, eyes wild and bloodshot. "You think she suffered?"

Marcus listened. In the silence, he did know what to think or say.

He didn't answer Andre. He only said, "We have to keep moving."

They did. They followed the stairs, wherever they led until it shifted into yet another hall, like the one Jasmine had found herself against the Bunny Man. It was as much a psychological torment as it was a physical ordeal.

They ran, not because it made sense but because it was all they had left. Marcus and Andre tore through the next corridor, every breath a knife, every step a bet against the odds. The air was viscous, the temperature swinging from freezer-burn to fever-dream within a single stride.

The hallway started tight, the walls so close the boys had to turn sideways to slip through, before abruptly bellying out into a bloated cavity lined with doors, each wide open. As they lunged for a door, it slammed shut out of reach. Each door Marcus tried was locked. He slammed his shoulder into them, but nothing yielded. The building seemed to laugh at the effort, each failed exit followed by a fresh bout of silence.

Marcus ducked through a threshold, Andre at his heels. The new space was an old office floor, the cubicles upended and scattered, their fabric panels ripped into confetti by years of water damage. The carpet squished underfoot, spongy with rot, but Marcus didn't slow. He weaved through the maze of half-walls and fallen chairs, Andre following on autopilot, eyes vacant but legs still pumping.

At the far end of the office, the Bunny Man stood half-swallowed by shadow, watching. Silent. Still. Marcus and Andre didn't wait to find out what came next, they kept moving.

The hallway pulsed, bulging and shrinking like the building's heart beat beneath the walls. Vents snapped shut, ceiling tiles fell like blades, stairwells vanished into blank walls. The Bunny Man didn't run—he didn't have to. His footsteps echoed, always near, never visible. At one turn, Marcus looked back.

The Bunny Man stood at the far end, eyes locked on them. He didn't hurry. He tilted his head, like a predator enjoying the kill's last sprint.

"Don't stop," Marcus panted. "Just—don't."

They careened forward, the walls pressing so close Andre's shoulder rubbed against the cinder block. At the next intersection, the way forward split. Marcus chose left, by instinct or luck, and nearly ran into a wall of exposed pipes.

"Dead end," Andre groaned, hands on his head, breath ragged as he paced in tight, anxious circles.

With no other place to go, they turned back they way they came, and instead of a long corridor, there was another door—this one slightly open, a cool refreshing breeze came from it, the promise of outside air behind it. Marcus grabbed the handle, though the door was already slightly ajar it was stuck in place. He heaved, then Andre joined, their combined effort finally popping it loose. They staggered through, and the door slammed shut with a thunderous clap.

Broken Glass

The next room was as big as the world. Or at least, bigger than anything left in Marcus's world. He and Andre staggered out of the door, side by side but not together, and found themselves on the raw production floor of ACME. The space yawned, black and endless, flecked with islands of moonlight that oozed through the broken skylight. What light survived spilled in a pattern of sharp parallelograms, catching on dust, glinting off the curved glass of shattered fluorescent tubes, and painting the concrete with bruised shadows.

Rusted sewing machines lined the wall, most toppled, their throats jammed with thread the color of nicotine. Mattress frames lay in heaps, tangled and collapsing in on themselves, the foam long since rotted away. At some point, a row of hydraulic lifts had buckled, and their arms now jutted out at strange angles, frozen in the act of hoisting nothing. It was quiet, not empty, but dense. A silence so heavy it pressed against their thoughts, thick enough to feel. Every footstep, every gasp, seemed to be consumed and digested by the concrete, leaving only the echo of effort.

Marcus stumbled, hit a puddle of grease, and barely kept his balance. He wheezed, the metallic taste of old blood in his mouth, and tried to orient. For the first time in minutes—

maybe hours—there was no immediate chase, no dragging of the Bunny Man's sledgehammer. Only the noise inside his head, the replay reel of their friends being broken, pinned, emptied out.

He turned, expecting Andre to be as grateful as he was for the reprieve. But Andre's face was wrong: gone was the cautious, skeptical mask; what remained was raw, desperate rage. His chest heaved, his shoulders bunched, and his fists opened and closed with the slow, steady rhythm of someone either fighting to stay alive or about to kill.

They stopped in a clearing beneath the skylight bathed in the moon light, where its beams hit pure, and for a second Marcus thought he saw himself reflected in Andre's stare—weak, out of ideas, and smaller than ever.

Glass crunched under Andre's boot. He spun, not looking at Marcus, but past him. His voice, when it came, was lower than usual, the words freighted with heat:

"This is your fault. All of it," he growled through clenched teeth.

It hit harder than any blow. Marcus opened his mouth, nothing came out but a thin dry rasp. "Dre, you saw what—"

"Yeah," Andre said, cutting him off. "I saw. I saw Jasmine get her head caved in. I saw Tasha turned into a fucking wall trophy. I saw D.T. get—" He broke off, the memory too fresh, too vivid. His hands came up, pressing at his temples, as if he could force the memory out through sheer pressure.

Marcus looked at his own hands, at the dirt and blood caked into every crevice, and tried again. "I didn't know. I never thought—"

"No, you didn't. Because you never do. You just run your

mouth, and we follow, because you're always so sure you got it." Andre laughed, a sound that cracked and died halfway out. "You said it was just a building. Just a dare. That it wasn't real. Jas...Jasmine was right, we shouldn't come."

Marcus tried to remember what he'd said, but it was all a smear—him, pushing, making jokes, dragging them deeper because to do otherwise would have been to admit he was scared. "I didn't mean for this to happen," he said, but even he heard the hollowness.

Andre spun on him, closing the distance so fast Marcus flinched. "You didn't listen. None of us ever listen. When somebody says a place is haunted, or cursed, or plain wrong, you know what you do?" Andre was shaking now, his voice climbing with every word. "You make it a joke. Because you think nothing bad ever happens to you. That you're invincible. And we—we go with it, because that's what you do. That's what you're good at. Leading."

He spat the last word like it was poison. Marcus wanted to say something—anything—but the only words that came to him were weak. "I'm sorry. I'm—."

Andre laughed even harder, then snarled. "The word Sorry is worth shit. It won't fix anything. Won't bring them back. It won't get us the hell out of here alive."

They were face to face now, the only thing separating them was air so thick you could've chewed it. Andre's eyes were wide, glassy, his jaw trembling as if it wanted to grind itself to dust. Marcus saw the tears before Andre did, and for a second he almost reached out, but his arms felt as useless as the broken lifts overhead.

Andre let out a breath, long and ragged. "You remember when we used to walk the tracks when we were kids? When it was you,

I and D.T? And whenever somebody saw us, they call security?" He didn't wait for a reply. "Now look at us. We're all that's left, and even now you're—" He shook his head, wiped his eyes with the back of his wrist. "—still trying to run the show."

Marcus swallowed, tasted blood, and shook his head. "I'm not trying to run anything. I...I want to live, Dre. That's all."

Andre's expression curdled. "Then start acting like it. Because the way I see it, if you keep making decisions, there won't be anyone left to live."

They stood, breathing hard, each waiting for the other to move. The silence in the factory grew heavier, settling in the cracks and corners, filling the space between them with memories that would never heal. Somewhere, deep in the shadows, something shifted—maybe a rat, maybe the wind, maybe the ghost of a scream still stuck in the duct work. But neither of them flinched.

Andre's knuckles whitened. "You ever stop and think maybe you're the reason it won't let us go?"

Marcus didn't answer. He knew there was no answer.

The moonlight shifted a hair, and it seemed for a moment that both boys had been erased, replaced by their shadows—long, stretched thin, merging on the dirty concrete like the outline of one lost thing.

The next breath Marcus took hurt worse than any of the wounds on his skin. He wondered if maybe that was what being alive meant now—enduring, even when the pain was all that was left.

"The Two of us can—"

Andre broke the stalemate first.

He stepped in and let it fly with a right hook, the punch was so hard it made the air pop. Marcus didn't have time to dodge; Andre's fist smashed into his jaw, the impact so clean it shut off the world for a second. Marcus staggered, arms pinwheeling, and crashed into a stack of old mattress frames. The pile collapsed with a scream of twisting steel, sending the rotten wood and busted springs across the floor in a miniature avalanche.

He landed on his back, vision fuzzing out in white static and for a second all he could do was stare at the ceiling, at the black line of exposed beams and the moonlight shivering between them.

Andre stood over him, chest heaving, eyes rimmed with red. "You think you're the only one who wants to live?" he spat. "You think you get to decide who dies?" His voice echoed in the room, bounced off the concrete in a way that made it sound like an accusation from all directions at once.

Marcus tried to sit up, but the pain in his jaw knocked him back. He blinked, found Andre's outline blurring above him. The argument was over now, there was no more room for words, only their next action.

For a moment, the world held still. Even the silence seemed brittle, as if a single noise might shatter it forever.

Then the noise came—a sharp, slicing whistle, followed by a wet thud.

Andre's scream, when it came, split the room.

A railroad spike had punched through the meat of his left calf, pinning him in place. The metal was old, black with rust. Before either could react, a second spike tore from the dark, slamming into Andre's right leg below the knee. The impact dropped him instantly, arms flailing as he crumpled to the floor

Marcus stared, disbelief muting every thought in his head. He'd seen violence before—fights in alleys, bad accidents on football fields, the occasional shooting—but never this, never the world reordering itself into something so cruel.

Andre tried to stand, but the spikes held. He twisted, howling, hands clawing at the metal, but it was as if the world had decided that this was how he would die. The blood came fast now, running in dark, syrupy ropes down the length of the spikes. It puddled at his feet and sprayed as he thrashed, painting the floor and the shattered mattress frames with long, arterial arcs.

Marcus forced himself upright. He tried to get to Andre, but his legs wouldn't cooperate, so he crawled instead, hands scraping over broken glass and splinters. He reached Andre just as the spikes lifted, jerking him into the air by some invisible force. Andre's body bent in half, righted itself, and hung upside down as if on a butcher's hook.

He dangled, the spikes holding him five feet above the floor. The blood now dripped in steady, fat drops, some hitting the concrete, some finding Marcus's face as he looked up in horror.

"Dre!" he shouted, hands reaching for Andre's flailing arms. He got a grip, tried to haul him down, but the spikes were rooted in suspended air, immovable. Andre's skin was cold already, the sweat and blood making it hard to hold on.

Andre's eyes rolled and focused. "Get it out!" he shrieked, voice gone two octaves higher than Marcus had ever heard it. "Help me—please—"

Marcus braced himself, tried to lever himself as he pulled on Andre's hand. Neither he nor the spikes budge. He pulled and pulled, ignoring the way the blood made his grip slick, and tried again. The effort sent a fresh gout of blood onto his forearm. Andre's screaming didn't stop, even when his voice cracked and went raw.

"Hold on, Dre. I got you. I got you, man," he said as he kept pulling, desperate, not knowing what else to do.

He didn't. Nobody did.

Andre's body trembled before stiffening. The blood now ran in thin streams, less forceful but more insistent, a faucet left open and forgotten.

"Dre, please," he whispered. "Don't—don't leave me alone in here."

Andre met his gaze, for a second, and something in that look made Marcus want to vomit. It was the look of someone who knew the end had already happened, that the rest was pain and waiting.

The blood kept coming, and Marcus kept pulling, until even hope was soaked and slippery and hard to hold.

When the next noise came—a dragging, metallic scrape, slow and deliberate—neither boy turned to look. They both knew what it was, who it was.

The Bunny Man was coming.

But for now, all Marcus could do was hold Andre's hand and wait for the world to finish what it started.

Marcus saw the shadow before he heard the hammer. It bloomed in the pool of moonlight, stretching out from nothing, gaining shape and edges with every step.

He barely had time to register the silhouette before a force like a football tackle hit him square in the chest. He left the ground, slammed into a tangle of metal and broken glass ten feet away. The landing split open the skin on his arms and cheek, sent shock waves down his spine. He tried to suck in air, but his ribs flared white with pain and the best he managed was a wet, rattling gasp.

The sound that followed was unmistakable: the low, dragging scrape of the Bunny Man's sledgehammer as it carved a line across the factory floor.

Marcus raised his head slowly, blood trickling down his neck, eyes huge and white with terror. The Bunny Man stepped out of the dark like he'd been waiting there all along. His coat in tatters, Stormy Kromer hat low over the void where a face should have been, hands black with old grease and murder. The sledgehammer looked heavier now, stained with a century's worth of grudge and rust and blood.

The Bunny Man didn't look at Marcus. He looked at Andre— still swinging, still alive, face twisted in the last expression he'd ever wear. The Bunny Man cocked his head, like a dog considering a crippled animal.

Then he lifted the hammer.

The world slowed down. Marcus watched as the Bunny Man braced himself, muscles coiled in his arms, and swung the hammer into Andre's ribs. The sound was a low, wet crunch, the noise of wood snapping under a tire, followed by a high, animal scream from Andre that no longer sounded like any human Marcus knew.

The next blow landed on Andre's thigh, splitting the meat and spraying blood in a long, arcing wave. The next hit snapped his shoulder backwards, so hard the joint exploded out of the skin and hung, pulpy and useless, over Andre's head.

The Bunny Man worked methodically, moving from limb to limb, pausing only to admire the handiwork before lining up the next shot. Andre's body jerked with every impact, and each time the blood flowed less, until at last there was only a thin drip, pattering down onto the frame of the mattress below.

Marcus tried to stand, but his body refused. He could only watch, every breath a torture, every blink bringing a new flashbulb image of Andre's destruction.

The Bunny Man finished with a blow to the head, shattering the skull and sending a mist of pink and bone fragments fanning out across the concrete. For a moment, the air shimmered, as if the violence itself had warped the space.

Andre's screams had stopped, replaced by a long, sucking silence.

The Bunny Man stepped back, looked up at the body, down at the sledgehammer. He gave it a little shake, as if to clear the residue, and turned to look directly at Marcus.

For the first time, Marcus understood the legend. The rage wasn't random—it was targeted, precise, personal. The Bunny Man wanted him to see it, to remember.

"Tragedies should be remembered," the Bunny Man's words echoed through his head.

Marcus tried to crawl away, but the glass dug in, each movement sending stabs of agony up his legs. He managed to make it a foot, two feet, before he heard the hammer drag behind him, closer and closer.

He didn't dare look back. He knew what he'd see: the silhouette, the hat, the empty face, the promise that it wasn't over yet.

Marcus made it to the edge of the moonlight before his arms gave out, his hands shaking too hard to support him. He turned, back to the wall, and watched as the Bunny Man advanced, each step measured and heavy.

For a second, Marcus thought he would die right there—pinned and broken, another slab of meat on the factory floor.

But the Bunny Man stopped. He leaned in close, close enough that Marcus could smell the rot and ozone and old rage. The hammer hung at his side, head down, like a man done with work for the day.

With a single, impossibly fast motion, the Bunny Man raised the hammer and brought it down on the metal frame above Marcus's head. The frame buckled, sent a fresh shower of blood and bone onto Marcus's face.

The Bunny Man waited, staring, as if daring Marcus to do something about it.

Marcus screamed, not because he wanted to, but because his body needed to remind itself it was alive.

The next sound Marcus heard was a sucking pop, like a bottle uncorking, as the Bunny Man summoned the spikes from Andre's body. The iron shot out of the ruined limbs and into the Bunny Man's outstretched hand with a wet, mechanical certainty, tearing new holes as they exited. Andre's corpse collapsed to the floor, landing with a thud so final it echoed in Marcus's bones.

The Bunny Man paused. He looked at Marcus, head cocked, the blankness of his face both invitation and threat.

Marcus met the gaze, just for a second. It felt like looking into a well so deep there was no bottom, only the knowledge that if he fell, he'd never stop.

The Bunny Man waited. Maybe he was giving Marcus a head start. Maybe he just wanted to savor the fear.

Marcus didn't stick around to find out. He scrambled upright, ignoring the pain in his hands and knees, and ran. He slipped twice in the blood, got his balance, then took off across the production floor, weaving between machines and piles of wreckage.

Behind him, the sledgehammer resumed its slow, steady scrape. The sound chased him down the rows, around corners, through doors that should have led to the loading dock but instead only opened into new, unfamiliar hells. Every time

Marcus thought he had lost it, the noise would come again, closer, insistent.

He didn't know how long he ran, or how many rooms he crossed, only that the world had shrunk to the circle of light in front of him and the certainty that if he stopped, the story would end the same as for everyone else.

At some point, the factory ran out of rooms. Marcus found himself back at the beginning with the first floor production area, the mattress graveyard, and where Andre had met his fate. Yet, there was no sign of blood, Andre's body, or even the Bunny Man himself.

He collapsed against a wall, lungs burning, vision flickering in and out. He waited for the hammer, for the silhouette, for the voice that would tell him it was all over.

But the only sound was his own breath, ragged and sharp.

He was alone.

For now.

Marcus pressed his forehead to the wall, shut his eyes, and tried to remember what it felt like to not be hunted. What it was like to have friends who warned of dangers?

He did not want to be the last one standing.

But he was.

And somewhere, in the dark, the Bunny Man was waiting for him to run again.

The Corpse in the Tunnel

Marcus couldn't bear the weight of solitude. He sprinted across the production floor, each footfall crashing into ghosts—Darnell's laughter, Tasha's sharp side-eye, Jasmine's weary sigh, Andre's endless comebacks. They surfaced in the darkness, unbidden, flickering and breaking like the dying bulbs overhead. He ran until the only thing louder than the Bunny Man's memory was the ricochet of his own heart.

The ACME Mattress Factory was infinite now, a box unfolding inside itself. Marcus weaved through the tangle of collapsed frames and upended sewing machines, cutting corners so sharp the rusted metal threatened to gut him. Every surface caught the light from his phone in a different way, warping it, chewing up the beam and spitting back a splatter of yellow and blue. He skidded past the row of hydraulic lifts—crumpled arms now stretching up like fossilized arms—and veered toward the corridor at the far wall.

The first door slammed behind him with a sound like a gunshot. The next door, ten yards on, waited until he was almost through, and slammed shut so fast it caught a slice of his shirt, nearly peeling him backwards into the dark. He ripped free, staggered, and kept moving, each new threshold waiting for him and slamming home with surgical precision.

The sound changed as he moved. At first, the doors barked in sequence—a warning, a countdown. By the fourth, they began to harmonize, a chord of heavy wood and hollow metal that reverberated down the spine of the building. Somewhere above, the bones of the place creaked, and Marcus imagined the Bunny Man at the center, pulling levers, playing the factory like a cathedral's organ.

He hit the stairwell at a dead sprint. The air in here was colder, sharper; it scraped his teeth, made his ears ring. The steps themselves sloped downward, the risers chipped and uneven, and after the first two Marcus lost count, just put his head down and let gravity have him.

The flashlight app on his phone had begun to stutter, the beam catching on the crumbling paint in bursts, revealing the stairwell as a throat lined with peeling skin. Each bounce of light uncovered something new: a child's sneaker, petrified with age; a soda can warped by heat; a puddle of something thick and brown, catching the light and turning it black. Halfway down, Marcus missed a step, slipped, and landed hard on his tailbone. The shock blasted a grunt out of him, and for a moment he just sat, gasping, unable to move.

"My fault," he croaked, and his voice, stripped of any bravado, ricocheted up the stairs and came back to him in a mocking chorus. "All my fault. They're dead because of me."

He didn't want to cry, but the body wanted what it wanted. The tears made the grime on his cheeks slick, and for a minute he pressed his head back against the wall, letting it take some of his weight, letting the cold soak in.

Above him, the stairwell pulsed with the heavy hush of abandonment. No footsteps. No voice, human or otherwise. For a moment, Marcus dared to believe that the thing in the hat had lost interest, that the Bunny Man had moved on to find other trespassers, other idiots who thought horror was just a game.

He wiped his eyes on his sleeve, which came away stained with sweat and blood from the cuts on his hand and face, and pushed onward. The stairs ended in a landing, where the emergency light was long dead, and the door at the bottom was already open, swinging lazily on one hinge, beckoning him to enter.

He hesitated, wanting to listen, to measure the silence for threats, but every inch of his brain screamed for movement. He ducked through the door, bracing for it to close on his heels, but this one just squeaked and hung there.

The basement corridor stretched out before him, a tunnel lined with forgotten machines and chemical drums that had rusted shut decades ago. Water dripped from the pipes overhead. Each drop hit with a sound exaggerated by the hush, sometimes landing on the concrete, sometimes on the back of Marcus's neck, cold and mean. The floor was slick, and at every step his sneakers made a new, inventive noise: the slap of water, the squelch of mud.

He kept the flashlight low, sweeping it back and forth across the floor. The beam danced over stains and shadows, sometimes catching on what might have been a footprint or a drag mark, sometimes just illuminating the endless debris of the factory's last gasp. The shadows chased him, growing longer and wilder each time the light flickered.

Halfway down the corridor, the phone's battery warning flashed, a red banner of doom. The light dimmed and rallied, but Marcus could already feel it failing in his hands. If it went out, there was no way he was going to find his way out in the dark.

He pressed on, muttering to himself, not even aware of the words. "It's just a building, it's just a building, you're smarter than this, keep your head, keep your head, don't let it win."

The mutter became a chant, not because he believed it, but because it was better than the quiet. Each new step seemed to drag him deeper, not just into the bowels of the ACME building, but into his own skull, where the worst parts of the night replayed on endless loop.

The corridor made a sharp right, a left, and straightened. The light caught on a bulkhead door, painted bright yellow, the warning stencils faded but still legible. Marcus tried the latch; it turned with a groan. He braced, expecting it to slam, but the door swung open so gently it might as well have been waiting for him.

On the other side, the world was colder. The walls here had sweated away their paint, leaving only the bare concrete, slick and pitted. The air tasted like pennies and old water. Marcus's breath came back at him in little puffs, each one visible, each one a countdown to when the light would give out and leave him blind.

He moved faster, half-skidding, always listening for the echo of footsteps behind him. But there was nothing—only the sound of water dripping, the frantic patter of his own pulse thumping in his head.

He pressed onward, the water getting deeper, the air turning from cold to freezing, when he reached an intersection, and for a moment—just a moment—the darkness felt less threatening. The water here was still, glassy, reflecting the dying light from his phone. He doubled over, hands on knees, chest heaving.

He stood there, blinking back the sting of sweat in his eyes, body shaking. He wanted to collapse, but the terror of what waited in the dark kept him upright.

"My fault," he whispered again. And in the thick hush, something—soft, distant—seemed to echo back in agreement.

For now, he was alone. But the question gnawed at him—why hadn't the Bunny Man come yet?

A sudden rush of cool air brushed against his skin, sharp and invigorating, as if he'd been trapped in the factory for an eternity. The scent of the nights fresh air, awoke something primal within him. With the dull light, he swept his gaze across the room, landing on a large drain set into the far wall. Moving toward it, he could feel the breeze whispering in from outside, a tantalizing promise of freedom that urged him forward.

A drainage tunnel. Maybe once meant for rainwater or chemical run-off. Now just a gullet, waiting to be fed.

He didn't hesitate. If there was a way out, even if it led to the sewer or to hell itself, Marcus was going to take it.

He dropped to his knees, and shined his phone into the mouth of the tunnel. The light went maybe four feet before it hit a wall of darkness. The space was tight—barely big enough for a grown man to crawl through—but that was all the invitation Marcus needed.

With the phone clenched between his teeth for light he entered. The first two feet were easy; the concrete gave way to corrugated steel, followed by a layer of wet sand and garbage that had been collecting for decades. With every move, his hands sank deeper into the sludge, he tried not to think about it. He kept crawling.

He crawled until his arms shook, a foot more, another, and just when he thought he would black out from the pressure and the stench and the fear of getting stuck, the tunnel widened.

He blinked the sweat from his eyes and shined the phone

ahead. The light caught on something pale. Something that didn't belong in a tunnel.

Marcus froze.

The pale thing resolved itself in the light, and it was a hand. A human hand, blue-white, clutching a chunk of rock as if in its last act of resistance.

He blinked again, but it didn't go away. He pressed forward, desperate not to see but unable to turn back.

The rest of the body came into view: the bones picked clean by time and vermin, but still more or less assembled in the position where the person had died. The hand, wrist, arm—all visible, the sinew long since stripped. The rib cage had collapsed, the vertebrae lined up like a row of dominoes. The pelvis and femur were stained brown, the marrow eaten out by water and age.

But it was the head that stopped Marcus cold.

The skull had been split, clean down the middle, as if by a blade or a sledgehammer. The two halves gaped apart, exposing the hollow where the brain had once been. The jaw hung open, teeth still clenched in a death ictus. And at the back of the skull, sunk deep into the bone, was a railroad spike.

Marcus's breath caught. He reached a trembling hand out, and brushed away the film of slime clinging to the top of the skull.

It was real. The spike had been driven in with such force that it protruded through the mouth. The skull had shattered around it, the bone peeling back like the skin of a fruit.

Next to the skeleton, almost reverently arranged, were the remnants of an old canvas jacket, its buttons eaten away. A Stormy Kromer hat lay folded beside the head, its ear flaps stiff with the residue of years underground.

At the skeleton's other side, nestled in the curve of its ruined ribs, was a sledgehammer. The handle was warped and chewed by water, but the head was unmistakable: heavy, pitted iron, still bearing the black stains of the work it had been made to do.

Marcus tried to speak, but the words died in his throat.

The Bunny Man. Or rather, the man he had been—buried here, murdered and hidden away like yesterday's trash. This was not a ghost story, not even a legend. This was a murder, and the rage of it had never left.

He stared at the corpse, at the railroad spike and the sledge-hammer, and he saw the truth of it, the echo that had been following him and his friends all night. He saw the face of the man who died here: not the blank, horror-movie mask, but the real one—tired, maybe, or desperate. And he saw how the world had forgotten, how the only justice left was violence and repetition, played out again and again in the factory's echoing dark.

Marcus shut his eyes, pressed his head to the slime-cold wall, and let the horror fill him. He had found the Bunny Man, and in doing so, he had understood that none of them had ever stood a chance.

He remained there for a beat, the stink of the tunnel clinging to his skin, the bones behind him and the darkness ahead.

He wondered if he would ever get out.

He wondered if, even if he did, he would ever be able to run again.

Though his body was telling him to just lay down and die with the bones, let the darkness crawl up and over him, become a rumor for the next round of idiot kids looking for a dare. Let the Bunny Man have his justice, even if it wasn't justice at all— just the mechanical re-enactment of violence, again and again, until someone remembered what had been done down here.

Yet, there was still a voice in him, smaller than before, raw and stupid and unkillable. It said: Get up. It said: Move. It said: Don't let this be the story.

So, he crawled. Leaving the remains of Clarence Brown behind and hopefully the factory with it. Vowing that if he were to survive, he would share all that had happened to him and friends until his last breaths.

He kept crawling, until his phone finally died completely. The screen guttered out, and for a moment the absence of light was so complete he nearly panicked, nearly screamed. But he didn't, because the only thing worse than total darkness was remaining still and being trapped with his thoughts.

Instead, he kept going. Blind, one arm forward, the other after. The tunnel floor sloped, rose, bent ninety degrees. He kept going.

There was a noise ahead—faint, but real. The sound of water, maybe. Or air, moving. Marcus followed it, hand after hand, foot after foot, until the wall of darkness broke, spilling into the city's glow at the tunnel's mouth. With the last of his strength, he staggered forward and burst into open air.

He tumbled hard, slammed onto his side, rolled twice, then skidded to a halt in the dirt and gravel. A blink, and the world snapped into color again: washed-out sky, pinprick stars overhead.

He was outside.

For a minute, he just lay there, cheek pressed to the cold earth, waiting for the hammer to start up again. It didn't. The only sound was the faint echo of traffic, very far away, and the pulse of his own blood in his ears.

He sat up. The air was cold, and the sweat on his body turned to ice. He shivered, arms wrapped around his knees, and tried to take it in: the city, the sky, the absence of anyone or anything but himself.

He looked back, over his shoulder. The ACME building loomed behind him, black against the patchwork of streetlamps and blinking tower lights. The third-floor windows were dark, but one at the very top—where the supervisors' offices had been—glowed with a faint, rotten yellow.

Marcus felt watched. Not by the ghost, but by the memory of what was left in the tunnel.

He tried to stand, but his legs buckled. He crawled instead, hands digging into the gravel lining the railway. He made it twenty feet before his body quit again, and he had to rest.

He laughed, once, a dry, splintered sound, at the absurdity of it all. He was alive, but only because the building had let him go. He wondered if it had done the same for anyone else. He doubted it. Was he allowed to survive for a reason?

He checked his arms. The right sleeve was covered in blood; the left was worse, the wrist swollen and hot. He flexed his fingers, pleased to see that they still worked, even if each movement sent a bolt of agony up the bone. He checked his legs—both covered in filth and streaks of red. He was pretty sure his knees would never be the same.

But he was alive. That counted for something.

The city lay ahead, cold and indifferent.

He staggered upright, swaying, and limped away from the tracks towards the gap in the fence behind the old market. It was three a.m. on the west side of Baltimore, the only witnesses the empty shells of row houses. No cars passed. No one called out from a porch. He walked, and every step made him feel less real, more like a ghost himself.

His mind drifted to Darnell, Tasha, Jasmine, and Andre, each name a weight, each memory a wound. He thought about how easy it had been to say yes to a dare, to make a joke of fear, to lead friends into the jaws of a story that nobody believed until it was too late.

He thought about the Bunny Man, the corpse, the spike, the storm of hate that still lived in the darkness of the old factory. He wondered if it would ever stop. He doubted it.

The city did not care. It would not care if he disappeared, or if he ran screaming down Lafayette Avenue until his legs snapped. It had seen worse. It would see more. In the end, he was just another smear on the concrete, another voice gone quiet in the night.

He walked, and the blood dried on his hands, and the sky went from blue to gray. He passed the corner where the streetlights finally caught up with him, and for a moment the world was almost bright.

He didn't stop. He didn't look back.

But behind him, the ACME Mattress Factory waited. It always would. The ACME building just sitting there waiting on the next person to make a dare.

The Last Knock

Baltimore at three in the morning was a wound that never scabbed. Streetlights fizzed out over Rayner Avenue, throwing stripes across the sidewalks and turning every window into a sheet of dull gold. Marcus limped the last two blocks with his hoodie pulled up, stained shirt clinging to the cuts on his arms, and his left shoe so caked with mud it slapped wet against the concrete. This was Baltimore and pain was as common as parking tickets.

He reached his front stoop and stood for a minute, head down, breathing in the cool air. The house was a brick twin, three windows across, dead hydrangea in a half-melted blue planter by the door. He twisted the front doorknob, surprised to find it ajar—an unusual oversight for his parents, especially in a city like Baltimore.

With just a gentle push the door swung open. Not wide—just a few inches, enough to show the dark slice of the hall and the old mail heaped on the floor, still unread since Friday. Marcus froze, the old warnings drilled into his skull: never leave the door unlocked. Not for five minutes. Not for a run to the corner store. It was the first rule of living on Rayner Avenue. His dad had said it so many times, he sometimes found himself dreaming of it, voice spooling through his skull like a skipping record.

But the door was open now. Maybe his dad was up early, maybe his mom forgot to shut the door after coming home from her shift. Maybe.

He listened. The house said nothing back. No TV, no clatter of pans, not even the old man's pre-dawn shuffle to the bathroom. Marcus let the cold air follow him in, one hand gripping the storm door, the other flexed at his side. The hallway stretched ahead with three framed photos. At the end, the stairwell rose in tight angles.

He called out, not loud: "Mom?" He waited a second. "Dad?" He tried to make his voice casual, a little annoyed. The way he always did.

No answer.

Marcus stepped inside, the door swinging half-shut. He braced for guilt, but a heavier dread lingered—the same one he'd carried from the factory, a gut-deep sense that the world had shifted without him.

As Marcus crossed the threshold, the door slammed behind him, its echo rattling through the empty house. Shadows twisted in the corners like secrets waking up. Heart racing, he charged up the narrow stairs, two at a time, each step pounding with dread. His room—once a refuge—now felt like a trap.

With trembling hands, he locked the door with a twist of the latch and promptly turned on the light.

"It's over," he muttered, though the words felt hollow against the oppressive silence.

The overhead light flickered, offering no comfort. It was cold, colder than it should be in the middle of spring, the kind of cold that crawled inside the bones and gnawed.

He sagged against the door and slid down to the carpet, knees to his chest, arms wrapped tight. The trembling got worse, a shudder that started at the base of his spine and radiated outward, rattling his teeth and fingers. He tried to squeeze it out, muscle against it, but it held fast.

Marcus pressed the heels of his hands into his eyes, desperate to block out the light and the room and the world, but all he saw was red static. All he heard was the memory of last night, the endless hammering, the wet, snapping crunch of bone and hope.

He whispered, not sure if he wanted to be heard. "Why is this happening?" It came out as a ragged cough, so he tried again. "Please. Please make it stop. Please."

The walls didn't answer. The world held its breath.

He tried to anchor himself with details—posters on the wall, an old pair of cleats dangling from the bedpost, the screen of his laptop glowing in sleep mode—but nothing held. The memories flooded in, breaking every dam he tried to build.

Darnell's scream, the one that didn't bounce off the walls so much as stick to them, the sound of a soul being uprooted.

Tasha, her legs buckled under her, eyes rolling white as the spike nailed her to the stairwell, blood turning the treads into a hellish slip-and-slide.

Andre, held aloft by nothing, skewered and left to bleed out in a slow, deliberate drip. His hands clawed at the air, not in hope of rescue but just to keep from being forgotten.

Jasmine, her face erased in one blow, the rest of her body turned to mulch by the hammer. She hadn't even screamed. Just a hollow look, a plea for forgiveness Marcus had no words for.

He made a noise, not quite a sob, more a dry heave. The guilt pressed into his chest, squeezing everything else out. He hugged his legs tighter, as if he could compact himself to nothing.

The cold grew sharper, more insistent. The overhead bulb flickered and stuttered. The light turned his skin sickly, shadowed the room in a strobing half-night. He pressed his face to his knees, tried to breathe through the fabric, but the air felt thin and sour.

Outside, the house was silent.

Then, slow as dawn, came the footsteps.

They started at the foyer, heavy and measured. Not the shuffle of his father's slippers, not the hurried cadence of his mom's late-shift exhaustion, but a plodding, relentless march. Each footfall had a reason, a slow count of doom.

Marcus's breath stopped. He listened, heart a rabbit's flutter behind his ribs.

The steps hit the base of the stairs, paused, then began the ascent. One. Two. Three. The treads creaked under the weight, each sound a miniature earthquake. The banister groaned, old wood straining against something it was never meant to hold.

Halfway up, the footsteps halted. Marcus clenched every muscle, willing the sound away, but it resumed, slower now, as if savoring each inch.

He wanted to scream, or at least to run, but his body betrayed him. He was stuck, a beetle pinned in place, watching the shadow under his door grow darker, thicker, more alive.

Then came the scrape.

Metal on wood. Slow, patient, drawing a line down the length of the hallway. Not a threat, but a promise.

Marcus pressed his face to his knees, eyes clenched, and whispered again: "Please. I'm sorry. Just—let me be." His voice barely carried over the hush, but he prayed it would be enough.

The footsteps stopped outside his room. The shadow at the

bottom of the door deepened, thick and oily. The doorknob rattled, just once, as if to test the lock.

Marcus's eyes opened, wide and wild. He stared at the thin line of orange light leaking under the door, watched as the darkness on the other side pooled and trembled.

He wanted to stand, to grab something, anything—a bat, a trophy, the old lamp by the dresser—but he stayed put, held by terror and the certainty that nothing he did would matter.

The scraping stopped.

A silence followed, worse than any scream. The doorknob twisted hard, the metal groaning. The hinges flexed, a low, mournful protest.

Marcus shivered, breath coming fast now, eyes locked on the door. The guilt in his chest twisted, then settled, heavy as a tombstone. He knew what waited for him on the other side.

But he didn't move.

He just sat and waited, like he always did.

Then the pounding started as a warning: three massive blows that rattled the hinges and drove splinters from the frame. The first made Marcus flinch so hard his neck spasm and caused him to jump up and away front the door, the second threatened to shear the lock straight from the door, and the third left a crack—a thin, spidering line—that ran from knob to threshold. He braced for the door to explode off its hinges.

There was nothing.

Marcus stood in the middle of his room staring at the door, heart doing double-time, body rigid as if the carpet might swallow him whole. He inched backward, one foot at a time, until his calves hit the bed frame. The lamp on the desk flickered in a stuttering pattern—on, off, on, then a final electric whine and darkness.

In the silence, he heard his own pulse, quick and wild. The air pressed in, colder still, and a thin line of breath curled from his lips.

He reached for the lamp, desperate for any weapon, but the cord jerked out of the wall and the base tumbled to the floor, rolling under the bed with a soft, final thunk. Marcus's hands balled into fists—useless, but better than nothing.

He stared at the door. Waited. Nothing.

Marcus spun at the darkness behind him, blind but knowing, and saw the silhouette against his bedroom window. The loom of him. A hat like rabbit ears, the breath of his shadow. A hammer raised slow as history. A voice like the grave:

"Tragedies should be remembered."

The hammer started its arc.

Marcus moved, but too late. The last thing he saw was the shape of the hat, the hollow of the eyes, the hammer blotting out the light.

The world went black, and stayed that way.

In the house on Rayner Avenue, there were no more footsteps. No more voices. Only the echo, lasting long enough for the city to forget.

But the legend, like all legends, waited for the next fool to knock.

Epilogue: Bodies on the Tracks

Mr. Johnson liked to arrive before sunrise, the only time when the Carver Vo-Tech's corridors were clean of voices. The school at this hour felt more like a mausoleum than a workshop— empty lockers, fluorescent bulbs clicking into consciousness one by one, the faint taste of lemon cleaner lingering in the air. He stood at the front door, sliding his ID through the cracked scanner, its whine too high for adults but punishing to the unprepared ear.

In his classroom, the silence was thicker. The desks—thirty blue plastic shells, each seat bolted to a steel frame that never sat flush—were all arranged in careful rows.

He turned on the lights, filling the room with the stuttering buzz and hum of old ballasts. From habit, he opened the window, though the spring air was cooler than he liked. He set his bag on his desk, poured coffee from his worn thermos, and smoothed the front page of The Baltimore Sun, on his desk.

The headline came like a punch: FIVE LOCAL TEENS FOUND DEAD NEAR ABANDONED FACTORY.

The font was too large, a circus trick for the benefit of whoever still bought paper. Mr. Johnson's hands went to his mug, fingertips blanching against the warmth, but he didn't drink.

He read the article slowly, not because the words were hard, but because the mind would not let them in all at once. The first paragraph was a summary, standard AP style. The bodies had been discovered at dawn by a CSX maintenance crew, scattered along the old railway spur that ran behind the ACME Mattress Factory. The word bludgeoned appeared three times before the second column.

He stopped, shut his eyes, and felt a brief, raw spike of nausea. He pressed his palm to the desk, waited for it to pass, then read again. The names were printed in bold, each one followed by a parenthetical age: Marcus Anderson (17), Tasha Williams (18), Darnell Thompson (17), Jasmine Mitchell (17), Andre Johnson (17). There were quotes from parents, a few from the principal, and then a long, speculative bit about what they believed happened to the teenagers.

Mr. Johnson set his jaw. He knew why.

He remembered Marcus's voice, the baritone flex a little too mature for high school, always eager to break the tension with a joke or a challenge. He remembered the way Tasha would roll her eyes but always have the answer, and how Darnell, always D.T.—could make anyone laugh, even when the subject was about death. Jasmine, who could out-argue the whole class, and Andre, the quiet one, who saw through everything but rarely said so. They were all gone now, pressed into newsprint.

He looked up from the paper and let his gaze wander the room. The wall clock over the whiteboard was stuck at 6:34, its second hand twitching with each attempt to move forward. He let the coffee rest, untouched, and picked at the edge of the paper, rolling it into tight spirals with his thumb.

The article continued. Police refused to comment on "the specifics of the wounds," but a source described the scene as "disturbing, even by homicide standards." It was the sort of line meant to feed the sharks at the morning meeting, but it landed with a wet, dead weight in the pit of his chest.

There was a sidebar. He read it because there was nothing else to do:

CELL PHONE RECOVERED AT SCENE: Police sources confirmed that a phone belonging to one of the victims was found "badly damaged but operational" near the site. The device contained several hours of video and audio recordings, most of which were "incomprehensible." The data is being analyzed by state investigators. Preliminary review found only static, fragments of conversation, and what one officer described as "bizarre, distorted audio that sounded mechanical or inhuman." The police declined to release further details, pending investigation.

He imagined the phone's last moments: a hand, shaking, camera held up to capture something—anything—in the dark. The voices, panicked. The recording running until the battery finally gave out. Mr. Johnson wondered if it was Tasha's phone. She had always been the most tech-literate, always ready to document proof of every insult and miracle. Or perhaps it was Marcus, filming for clout. Or Darnell, hoping to catch one last joke.

He looked at the empty seat in the third row, the one Marcus had claimed and defended with exaggerated outrage whenever anyone tried to take it. The desk still bore the faint outline of the word LEGEND, scratched in with a house key and then laboriously blacked out with permanent marker when Mr. Johnson caught it. Now the letters seemed like a memorial.

He read on, searching for blame. There was none, at least not in print. No mention of drugs, no hint of a gang hit.

The next paragraph referenced the factory's history, noting

the rash of accidents and fires in the 1960s, the shuttered windows and razor wire, the faded graffiti that ringed the loading docks. The article finished with an obligatory call for anyone with information to contact the tip line. Mr. Johnson doubted that anyone would.

He set the paper aside and pressed his hands flat to the desk, feeling the slickness of sweat. He drew a long breath, but the air caught in his throat, stayed there, and turned to something sour.

He replayed the last conversation he'd had with Marcus, only days ago. The boy had hung back after class, grinning the way he did when he wanted something. He'd asked about "urban legends"—whether any of them had a grain of truth.

Mr. Johnson remembered how he'd laughed, soft and indulgent, the way teachers do. "Every city's got stories, Marcus. They're all built on somebody's real pain, somewhere. You just have to dig for it." He'd meant it as a warning, or maybe as encouragement to find his own stories—he couldn't remember now.

But Marcus had taken the answer in stride, eyes bright. "So you think it's real? Like, could it really happen?"

Mr. Johnson remembered the chill, the way it had seemed to settle around the boy like a premonition.

He should have told him not to go.

He gripped the edge of the desk until his hands hurt, knuckles white. The skin on his forearms was stippled with goose bumps. He let the coffee sit, a ring of neglected warmth spreading across a stack of ungraded worksheets.

He turned away from the desk, walked to the window, and stared at the schoolyard, half-obscured by the steam of his breath. The city looked the same—buses idling at the curb, early smokers pacing in clumps—but everything felt wrong.

Before he knew it, the bell rang with a violence reserved for emergencies. Mr. Johnson jerked away from the window, hands numb where they had pressed the glass. He took a second to center himself, breathing in the bleach and the dust and the industrial odor of old hope, then turned back to his classroom.

Students trickled in. At first, just a pair of boys from his second-period, heads down, voices tamped to a near-murmur. They dropped their bags at the far side of the room and watched him with the wary, side long glances usually reserved for substitutes or the day after a fire drill. After them came two more—girls this time, both wrapped in the same Carver Vo-Tech hoodie, sharing a phone between them but not, today, a word. The rest came in clusters, never more than three at a time, filling the space with silence and the briefest flutters of anxious energy.

No one looked directly at Marcus's desk. But Mr. Johnson saw the way they circled those absences, the way a finger might skirt the edge of a wound. Some students placed their things extra quietly. Some sat early, hands folded, eyes on the wall. Others hovered in the back, it was certain that there was something odd in the air.

Mr. Johnson watched, cataloged each face, and found himself doing the mental roll call out of habit. Every missing name was a gap in his own chest. His hands wanted to fidget—flick the edge of the grade book, smooth the papers into perfect stacks—but he held them still at his sides, a last-ditch attempt at dignity.

He let the silence build, waiting for the clock to catch up with the truth.

At 7:15 sharp, he stood, the motion slower than usual. He pushed his chair back. The scrape of wood on tile shot through the room, and for a second every eye lifted to him, including those that had planned to look nowhere but the floor.

He wanted to say something. Anything. There were words he'd rehearsed in his car, words the guidance office had offered, all about community, and loss, and how "sometimes the world hurts so hard we can't explain it." But none of it fit. None of it matched the sick, greasy knot that filled the air.

He crossed to the whiteboard, uncapped a marker, and wrote in a hand so steady it surprised him: "REMEMBER Tragedies."

The cap snapped back on, a sound so crisp it seemed to echo.

He turned, faced the room. The fluorescent tubes overhead flickered, pulsing with the breathless syncopation of a dying star. The shadows along the window wall deepened, then evaporated. His own voice seemed trapped somewhere behind his sternum.

He scanned the desks, the nervous faces. He let the moment stretch, elastic and cruel, until finally he spoke.

"We lost some of our own the other night," he said, and the words tasted like blood.

A hush. Even the HVAC stilled, as if the building wanted to listen in.

"They were here with us not long ago. Some of them were in this room." He gestured, not to the empty desks, but to the windows, the ceiling, the world outside—anywhere but the holes left behind. "They won't be coming back. And that's not fair, or right, or easy to understand. But we're going to keep going."

A soft intake of breath from the back, maybe a sob. He let it pass, and didn't try to fix it.

He swallowed, feeling the words catch in his throat.

"If you want to talk, I'm here. If you need a break, take it. If you want to remember, do it however you need to."

He stopped there, unable to say more.

The bell rang again, softer now, as if it too had lost the will to shout.

He let the class settle, let them whisper, let them look or not look at the empty chairs. He watched the sunlight slide up the far wall, a thin, colorless ribbon inching its way toward the future.

He wondered how long it would be before the city forgot, or at least pretended to.

He wondered how many more stories the world needed before it got the lesson right.

He wondered, most of all, if he would ever be able to sleep through the night again.

Above him, the lights flickered on, and the day began.

Afterword

Image 1 of Acme Mattress Company near corners of Lafayette Avenue and Bentalou Street.

Image 2 of ACME Mattress Company

Overgrown entrance into ACME

Image 1 of train tracks beneath bridge beside ACME heading south.

Image 2 of train tracks beneath bridge beside ACME heading north.

Lafayette Bridge facing west with ACME looming in the distance top right hand corner.

ALL PHOTOS TAKEN BY THE AUTHOR.

Stormy Kroger Rail Worker Hat

According to Maryland Department of the Environment:

Site Location:
The Acme Business Center is located at 2120 West Lafayette Avenue in the west south central portion of the City of Baltimore, MD in the Gwynns Falls drainage basin. The property consists of five lots on three blocks

and measures a total of 8.42 acres. The Acme Business Center area is bounded by Bentalou Street on the west, Winchester Street on the north, Lafayette Avenue on the south, and the Amtrak right-of-way on the east. The 8.42 acres of property within the scope of this investigation incorporates five parcels of land currently owned by 2120 West Lafayette Avenue Limited Partnership.

Site History:

Dating back to at least 1914, the area has been primarily commercial/industrial in nature. Historic records indicate a uniform use of these parcels dating back through the mid-20th century. Sanborn Fire Insurance maps from 1914 through 1953 detail utility pole processing and storage, and grocery and dry goods related companies occupying the properties of concern. Sanborn Fire Insurance Maps of the era detail grocery warehouses covering much of the area of concern. In the more recent past the Acme Corporation, a retail grocery operation, has operated out of the buildings in the area. Founded around 1918 as a cooperative venture by several grocery store chains in Philadelphia, the American Stores Company eventually converted most stores to the ACME brand. The Company ceased to exist upon its acquisition by the Albertson's grocery store chain in 1999.

see: Microsoft Word - Acme Rosemont.doc
more articles: After 18 years of ownership, city sells a derelict industrial complex for $1 | Baltimore Brew

Also by Willie Gibbs

The Hole: Book One

Experience and relive The Hole, it is a true inspiring story in which a young man desperately struggled to overcome The Hole. To him the streets of Baltimore city was The Hole, it was a place that had bind and consumed his life, it gave some but took more. Surviving in the streets he had to watch as the drug game sucked many of his friends and family down into its dark abyss like the black hole it truly was. Finally realizing after years of tribulation and lost, he came to find that the key to his redemption lay in a form least expected.